THE MYSTERY MAN FOUND

TULSI DAVEY

Dedicated to:

To all the delusional beings,
especially the ones who dare to dream and live life
like a main character.

To the people in my life,
who make me smile, support me, and
brings me joy, a big thank you.

Contents

Contents

About The Author

Tulsi Davey is musician living in Vadodara, India. She was brought up in Surat. This is her first book, *the mystery man found. It's a* rom-com novel, published when she was fifteen.

Her interests are as diverse as the culture of India. She loves to do music composition, write poems, stories and analyse human behaviour.

She holds a *madhyama poorna* certificate in classical music from ABGMV Mandal, Mumbai. She studies in 11th grade currently (2024) and has opted for the stream Humanities.

She loves composing music, travelling and spending time in the presence of Nature.

As a passionate musician, she finds solace in composing music that resonates with the diverse rhythms of India.

Her love for nature and its serenity has taught her the value of patience, observation and simplicity. With her debut book,
'*The Mystery Man Found*', Tulsi Davey invited readers to embark on a journey of discovery, exploring the complexities and beauty of human experiences.

Tulsi Davey is a young aspiring music composer with a burning passion to preserve the rich heritage of Indian classical music. Hailing from the culturally vibrant cities; Vadodara and Surat. With a deep respect for the Indian traditional music, she is dedicated to creating music that not only honour the classical traditions but also innovate and experiment with fusion sounds.

As a writer, Tulsi's love for music influences her storytelling, and often waves musical themes that motif into her narratives. Her writing and music are intertwined, reflecting her passion for the arts and her desire to share the beauty of Indian culture with a wider audience.

Acknowledgements

Hi all!

I cannot possibly thank everybody who has contributed to this book. You guys know who you are and at what parts you contributed in. So, in case if I missed out, I'm really sorry.

The ones I would like to specially thank are:

God, for giving me so much.

My parents, for raising and encouraging me.

My friends, for accepting me the way I am.

Special gratitude to the people who noticed me through this book; and to all those who provided support, read, offered comments, remarks and assisted in improving this book.

I am forever grateful to the following individuals who have supported me through this journey of writing 'The Mystery Man Found'.

First and foremost, to my mother, Shraddha Davey, thank you for being my rock, always encouraging me to pursue my dreams and reminding me of the person I aspire to be.

To my father, Chetan Davey, thank you for being my backbone and the biggest cheerleader. Your excitement and enthusiasm for this book were contagious, and the constant queries about the next chapter kept me motivated.

A very special thank you to Khushi Patel, a dear friend who helped me finalize and edit the cover page. Your creative input and friendship are invaluable.

A big thank you to another very dear friend, Dev Kanani, My brother who keeps on encouraging me to achieve my dreams and never misses to appreciate when I achieve them. Your patience and eagerness to read my work have meant a lot.

To my dearest childhood friend, Prisha Parmar, thank you for standing by my side and accepting me the way I am. Studying together till 10th to parting ways due to different streams. Thank you for still supporting me.

To my English Teacher, Murali Mohan Sir, who edited 'The Mystery Man Found', forever grateful to him. His guidance and feedback have been instrumental in shaping this story.

Lastly, I extend my heartfelt gratitude to all of you for giving so much of love to my first book. Dear Readers, You mean a lot to me. Thank you for being a support system. If you enjoy reading this book, I would consider my task complete.

Tulsi Davey,
20th July 2024

CHAPTER ONE

Teenage Love

Amidst the chaos of life, survived a young girl. As calm as a lake and deep like a sea. She was sixteen wondering how it must be like to grow up and live a beautiful fairy tale. For her, life was a blockbuster film and she was the lead character. She believed that her prince charming is being trained somewhere in some quarter of the world. And so was the young lady. The young lady was romanticising life at her fullest. She used to add background music to every single thing. When she studied, she played soft instrumentals, in the evening while cycling she played pop romantic songs, at the time of cooking she added country music. And when she slept she used to listen to some old evergreen melodies. She had composed a playlist on things that had happened in her life. And of course why not? She was a Taylor's girl.

In the month of July, I met a guy. He was the head boy of the school. Tall, handsome and popular but still a poindexter. He was one of the greenest flag I had met.

"Aarohi!! Watch out, Mr.T's right there in the next corridor" a baritone voice came from behind. He was Nishit from 11th Science.

"Oh thanks *bhaiya*, I was wondering where the physics laboratory in charge must be. I wanted to return him the resistor I borrowed during the practical"

"Oh he's in the principal's cabin. Give it to me. I'll return it. I've a session in the next lecture.

"Thank you."

"SURE" said Nishit.

I returned back to the classroom. The girl next to me asked in a whispering voice, "Who was he?"

"Who?" I asked back.

"The tall, handsome guy you were talking to."

"Oh, that guy!! Senior Head boy"

"Oh Okiee"

The same evening I met Nishit at the veggie market. He looked stylish in his grey track pants, black tee, and cool headphones draped around his neck. His black metallic-framed specs added a touch of sophistication. From a distance of about five meters, I waved at him, but he didn't notice.

I went a little further and shouted "NISHIT, HEYYY" Nishit turned around looking bewildered and then his eyes lit us as he saw me.

Nishit greeted me with a warm smile and said

"Hello, you look pretty" I blushed and replied with a simple "oh thanks" I was wearing a crisp white knee-length dress, and my hairs was braided neatly. I couldn't help but wonder what specifically caught his attention- was it my dress, my hair, or something else? But I decided to brush off the compliment and ignore the flutter in my chest, focusing on the conversation instead."

"You wear glasses?" I asked, curious. 'Yes,' he replied, 'but I don't wear them to school. I don't want to be labelled a nerd.' I chuckled and said. "HAHA, you look great with them! You should wear them to school too." I wanted to return the compliment after he called me pretty. His face lit up with a smile, clearly pleases with my comment. As we continued shopping, I noticed he was different from other boys. He was confident and savvy, knowing just how to bargain, and even brought his own reusable white cloth bag. After we finished shopping, we decided to treat ourselves to ice cream at the nearest parlour"

"We sat together at the ice-cream parlour; enjoying our treats- he had a classic butterscotch cone, while I savoured a sweet mango flavoured candy. As we lingered for almost half an hour, our conversation flowed effortlessly, delving into the depths of life. He shared with me his passion for cooking dinner for his family, his dreams, his ambitions and how he spends his free time. It was a pleasant and meaningful exchange. But soon, glanced at his watch and mentioned he had to leave.

We bid eachother farewell and parted ways, heading to opposite direction. As I walked home, my mind begins to wander- how wonderful it would be if he was my boyfriend? I hadn't developed feelings for him yet, but couldn't help indulging in those fanciful thoughts. Suddenly, my inner voice scolded me: 'AAROHI, stop!! You've always called him "*bhaiya*". Don't be ridiculous!"

Next day, I was sitting in the school canteen when Nishit approached me, carrying a plate of steaming *upma*. He was wearing his specs again, this time with an air of complete confidence. I couldn't help but wonder if he had worn them because I had called him cool the day before. But I pushed the thought aside and focused on the present moment. "Have some" he offered, holding out the plate. I hesitated, feeling a twinge of guilt for refusing, but I knew I couldn't accept. As a member of an average Indian family, I had been taught that sharing meal with a boy who wasn't a close friend or family member wasn't proper. So, I politely denied. We spent the next few minutes gossiping about our teachers and sharing laughs. As a head boy, Nishit had the inside scoop on all the school's secrets, and I enjoyed hearing the stories.

"hahha, you have the benefits of being the head boy's best friend." He said with a grin. I repeated the words "Best friend....?" in a slow murmuring voice, my eyes locked on his. He caught the hint of surprise in my tone and his face showed flicker of regret. " Uhh, I mean, you're a good friend," he corrected himself. I replied with a simple "OHh" trying to sound nonchalant.

As the bell rang, signalling the end of the break, students started dispersing to their classes. Nishit was still sitting there, finishing his plate of *Upma*. He asked me if I was getting late for my classes, but we ended up walking out together anyway.

As we parted ways, I couldn't shake off the thought: "Did I just fall for him?" I asked myself. "Uhh, noo, Aarohi, not at all." But my mind countered with: "But he's such a nice guy. Come on, Aarohi, he's not the one." I tried to reason with myself, but my thoughts were a jumbled mess.

Just then, Lilly chimed in: "Aarohi, are you sure he's just a friend?" I was taken aback by my own doubts and replied in a harsh voice: "Please, Lilly, don't distract me!!"

Saying this I did not spoke a single word till 2o'clock. On the way to home, I kept thinking whether I like him or not but nothing gave me an a answer

It was 3a.m, I realised that I've actually started liking Nishit. Not just his smile, His looks, His personality, His grades. But also, His way of acting towards others, He used to gratitude about every single thing, The way he cooks dinner for his family, The way he goes to buy vegetables every evening. He was a complete green flag. And I realised it. I immediately called Lilly, yes in the middle of the night,

I called her without having a second thought.

"Helloooo" she said in a lethargic, sluggish voice. "BITCH I LOVE HIM."

"LOVE WHOM?"

"Nishit."

"OH....OH MY GOD, I KNEW IT!!!!!" she said with enthusiasm.

"So...what now?" she added.

"UHhh.. do you think he likes me back?"

"well, I don't know. Let's find out." She said.

The next day, Lilly and I spotted him in the canteen and decided to sit at the table next to him.

"Heyy Aarohi, morning! He said with a warm smile. My heart skipped a beat as he told me how much he loved my voice, revealing that he watched my Instagram videos the previous night. "You sing great" he added making me blush. I stuttered out, "th-th-thankyou feeling nervous and flustered. Who wouldn't be, after all? He was no longer a 'Bhaiya' to me. He was my crush.

Later, during our mathematics lecture, Lilly leaned over and whispered, 'Girl, I'm telling you, Nishit likes you too!' I raised my eyebrow, intrigued . "Oh really?" I asked, trying to sound nonchalant.

"Yes bro! Didn't you see the way he was praising you? So sweet of him." I rolled my eyes laughing, 'Shut up, it's like a blind leading a blind!' I teased, trying to downplay the excitement building up inside me.

"C'mon Lilly you cannot decide that with a mono compliment. Don't give me hopes." "Okay fine, let's observe more".

"That same evening, I received a text from Nishit- a voice note that sent my heart racing! I completely lost my chill, letting out a loud, excited like a wild animal. I started around, imagining fake scenarios of our wedding, with Bollywood music playing in the background. I couldn't wait to hear what he had to say, but I decided delay the pleasure, letting the curiosity build up. An hour later, I finally opened the voice note, and my heart skipped a beat- he was singing!!

A bollywood romantic song, no less! While he wasn't the best singer, his low, resonant voice made up for it! I fell for him all over again! Not knowing how to reply, I decided to praise his voice instead of his skills. After all, he was my crush, and I couldn't help but be biased!

"Mannnnn! You have a beautiful voice. It's so professional. I'm in love with it." I replied. "Thank you madam" he said.

MADAM??? It was the first time a guy had called me that. I was falling for him more and more.

***

"He called you madam, he definitely likes you. Trust me" shouted Lilly to fit that thing in my brain.

"LILLY, Even I think that. But you cannot assume things just like that." I explained.

"Just like that? Aarohi he calls you Madam, he shares things with you, HE SENT YOU A VOICE NOTE. You really think this is JUST FRIENDS behaviour?" She shouted again.

"Well, okay fine... What do you think, I should do now?

"GO CONFESS BABES"

"co...Confess? Are you out of your mind? What if he rejects??? What if this confession ruins our friendship??? What if he starts hating me?? What if..."

"SHUT UP" Lilly interrupted.

"Just go and say it out, don't over think. The worst he could say is NO. And he would not say that. You're beautiful, Intelligent, Courteous and such a wife material.

No smart guy would reject you."

"Ohm Lilly, I love you!"

"I love you too babes, He'll say that" "BAHAHA".

I had known Nishit for four months, and confessing my feelings seemed too soon. Anyone would be taken aback! Lilly constantly encouraged me to take the leap, but fear held me back. What if he rejected me? After six months of one-sided love, I finally gathered the courage to ask him out. 'Umm... Nishit.. I want to say something', I began, my voice trembling.

'Oh?' he replied, his tone nonchalant. I needed reassurance. 'Nishit, I think I like you', I confessed, my heart racing.

He chuckled, 'Aarohi, you said you "think" you like me, you're not sure about me, hahaha!' His joke caught me off guard, but I was relieved that the mood remained light.

'Nishit please!! I'm fucking serious!' I emphasized, my eyes pleading. He laughed again, 'If you're serious, you should go to the hospital' I rolled my eyes,

'Omg , sorry for these lame jokes!' I glared at him, my eyes sharpening and giving him KEEP-YOUR-MOUTH-SHUT stare.

He understood, backing off with a sheepish 'sorry madam'.

I calmed down as he called me 'madam.' I asked, 'Nishit, i said I like you. Do you want to say anything, or should I go? He replied, 'Aarohi you're really nice girl. I won't give you false hopes like others but listen this carefully,

My heart sank, unsure of what to say, so I just nodded. He continues, "You like me because you've met me recently, but you'll meet many people in the future. Only then you can decide who you really love. I know you're a curious girl eager to find your perfect match, but have patience. I want you to date the best. Admire your thoughts, admire your mysterious prince, adore it, appreciate it, and focus on your studies. You're just sixteen and you know what? Education is the key to date the best. The more educated you become, the better you'll be at choosing the right person. It's that simple.

His words poured out like a gentle rain, and I found myself swept away by his eloquence. His long speech was like a balm to my soul, soothing my doubts and fears. His explanation was a wake-up call, inspiring me to see things from a new perspective. And in that moment, something shifted inside me. I felt a transformation taking place, like a caterpillar emerging from its cocoon as a beautiful butterfly. I became a new version of myself, reborn sense if purpose.

"Nishit, this is amazing! Where did you get those dialogues from? Oh my god!" I exclaimed, my eyes wide with wonder. He chuckled and replied, 'Uhh, I said all that to fulfil my bollywood dream. The only thing missing was the background music, haha!"

His response made me laugh, and I couldn't help but admire his creativity and sense of humour.

We both had an endless laugh that day. It was our best conversation. And I wasn't disappointed at all that he rejected me. Rather, I was satisfied that I had such great friends like him.

I told the whole thing to Lilly next day. "OMG Aarohi, You guys make such a great couple. I swear, both of you are made for eachother. Cuz you talk about things that go above my head." "Shut up, you were right, the worst he could say was no. But he chose to say the best."

"Awwwwwww, Aarohi in loveeeee".

From that day, My goal was to be the most successful one in the family. It wasn't easy but it was worth it. There was a woman I wanted to be. And until I reached that point, I had work to do. I starting planning timetables, I started studying more and started romanticising my life. In reality, I fell in love with myself.

CHAPTER TWO

London

I started visiting library for self study. It had become my comfort space where I used to find peace. It was a place where I used to know myself.

It was my 'me time' when I was in library and nobody dared tom disturb me. It was a vintage styled library, which had millions of books. I always wondered, if anybody had read all of the books and the question was still unanswered. Time flew really fast. Lilly got shifted to Delhi for her higher school. Nishit disappeared. He got graduated from the school and now was off to college. I had lost contact with him. I wish we were in contact. I wanted to talk with him for hours and then I remembered I had work to do which was going to last forever. Lilly and I were now long distance besties. She talked to me about her new school, new classmates, the new city and of course we used to gossip.

After Lilly got shifted and disappearance of Nishit, all I used to do was Wake up, go to school, return, study, visit library, sit on the river bank, return home, sleep and repeat. In the evening, after my self-study sessions in the library, I used to visit the river front and sit for hours in silence. Listening to music, Adoring my future boyfriend. Wondering when would he enter into my life.

My life was a complete bollywood movie without a hero. I was a hopeful romantic. All I had was hopes. Hopes to find the best in the world.

I wanted to be called as a Neuropsychologist. I was a girl who believed that mental health shouldn't be taken for granted because, mental health exists and it is as important as physical health. Little miss, had decided to aware people about mental health when she was in 8th grade.

After passing my board exams I could't wait to study about psychology. I was happy that I would never ever have to study MATHS and SCIENCE again. But god had different plans. There I was, studying STATISTICS. It was not that bad but I never liked maths. So, for me it was the worst thing.

I used to miss Nishit. Lilly and I didn't even know whether he was in India or not. Until one day, a notification popped up in my cell phone.

"nishitshah_03 has requested to follow you". I almost screamed. I was in the library. Everybody took an attention towards me. For the first time. Since I ever started visiting that place. Again I decided not to accept it straight away. I choose to complete my work first. It took me bloody two hours. Later, I had to buy comestibles which my mom had ordered me to do and finally, I was home after 4 hours. It was a really hectic day. I had to visit to the main city area with tons of lorries, cars, bikes, dust and a hugeeeeee traffic jam.

And ofcourse why not? It was the main 'kissanmandi' of the city. I had to survive between some dangerous aunties who were constantly pushing each other with their butts. Anyways, Finally, I was home. Safe and sound. I took a warm bath, had dinner and got straight into the bed. I had completely forgot about Nish's follow request until I started scrolling.

"Accept" I clicked. I started scrolling again. After 15mins, I got a text from Nishit. "Hey Aarohi! What's upp. Long time no see"

"oh, look who's saying. The one who disappeared. Changed the contacts and deleted all social media platforms. Hats off sir" I replied.

"HAHA I'm in London. Doing medical. Got scholarship and here I'm. What are you doing these days? And how's Lilly?" he replied back

"Lilly got transferred to Delhi for her high school study. And here I'm at the same old place on some new shit. I'm all alone now. I miss you and Lilly so much. I was still in contact with her but you completely disappeared. Can I know what did you take to get in touch with me?" I said

"OMG Aarohi, calm down. I didn't inform anybody because the decision was taken all of a sudden. I had to apply for the student visa. I had to shift. I had to find a good part-time job. Things were very messed up. After settling, I had my own routine started and couldn't find time to contact anybody." He explained

"OH- It's okay Nish, I understand. It's been two years now. You liking it there?" I asked

"Well, kind of. I mean it's great until you start missing the traditional street food wala. Specially Panipuri. I really miss those little things that are not so little."

"HAHA, I get it. But why don't you visit India. Your parents are here. You should visit atleast once a year."

"I did, I did visit last Diwali. They took me to the village for farming and meeting relatives. Which I really enjoyed"

"Ohh- that's greattt." I replied.

As we bid eachother adieu, I returned to the monotony of my daily routine, where the tedium of waking up to a sea of textbooks and notes threatened to consume me whole. The days blended together in an endless blur of study and repetition, punctuated only by the occasional declaration of affection from my besotted classmates- declarations I politely but firmly rebuffed, my heart already pledged to the one who would one day be my husband.

Even I didn't knew what I was doing but I was liking it. And if I like it, It doesn't need to make sense to others. Right? I kept rejecting all the boys who proposed me. Until one fine evening I saw Nishit's post with a girl. Hand in hand.

She was tall. Her short hair framing a face that radiated a warm, fair- skinned glow. Her height eclipsed mine, stirring a faint whisper of insecurity within me. Yet, it was her eyes that truly set her apart- safe, gentle and profound, like a tranquil oasis in a world of turmoil. Her beauty was not the fleeting, superficial kind and plastered on billboards, but a robust, authentic loveliness that seemed to emanate from the very core of her being, leaving the artificial charms of the world's princesses to pale in comparison.

Nishit was in a dark green kurta, he still had those deep unfathomable golden brown eyes where you could get lost if you stared long enough.

Beside him was that girl, Taller than me, wearing a floral saree which really looked good but let's just pretend that it was average, a gajra and a small black bindi on forehead which made her look even more beautiful. Nishit had tagged her on that post. "vidhyasharma".

I hope they both are cousins. GOD PLEASE! I opened her profile and what I saw didn't justify Vidhya as Nishit's cousin SISTER. Still I chose to text Nishit and ask her who was she. THE GUTS!

"Hey, Aarohi! She's my girlfriend. We met eachother in the second year of university in the feast. She's in the HR department of commerce and finance. It's been a year now of our relationship." He texted

I was broken. I didn't have feeling for him anymore until I saw him with some other girl called Vidhya. Vidhya was really pretty. She was far better than me. I was a brown girl, with long hairs, and average heighted. I was not happy but I didn't have any other option. All I can do was praise that couple.

"OH-that's so cool. She's really pretty. You both look great. Touch wood. Does your parents know about her?"

I couldn't stop myself from asking that question .

"Yes, they do. They like her. And so does hers. They like me as well. They find me a decent guy" he replied

"Decent guy?? And you?? Oh really??" I tried not to look jealous. And I guess I succeeded.

"C'mon of course I'm! Even Vidhya doesn't buy it. What's gotten into you guys!" he said.

VIDHYA. There's no doubt. I have to make a habit of this name now. There's a third person in our conversations. Who is being given all the priority. Oh wait- I am the third person actually. How dumb I'm.

"VIDHYA IS RIGHT, no arguments. I'll talk to you later. I've work to do"

"Sure.".

I was broken. Completely shattered. I didn't defeated when Nish rejected me but I surely felt it when I saw Vidhya with him. I didn't sleep the whole night. I was daydreaming about my future husband. *The mystery man.*

Next morning, I bunked my school. I was at the library. The whole day. *Studying, studying and more studying.* Imagine how hurt one must be that they start to study more. From that day I made myself really busy. I never opened social apps again. I started listening to Arijit Singh and Taylor Swift. I had disappeared.

I told about this to Lilly and she told me to block him. HUH... crazy bestfriends.

"This is not possible. How can I just block him for no reason. That's really rude."

"Why not? You have to."

"No, I'm not going to"

"Okay then go die. Keep crying for someone who doesn't even care"

Lilly got logic. But I preferred not to block him. Afterall, I always do what I want to do.

CHAPTER THREE

New Beginnings

Time flies. I was in 12th grade now. I had my board exams once again. Solving sample papers, giving tests, attending revision classes is all that I was doing. I had my Board after 3 months and I had completely forgotten about Nish, Vidhya, London and stuff. All I knew was to score the highest to get admission in the best college. I had a timetable with my mom used to make me follow STRICTY.

7:00- 8:00 Morning Chores
8:00-11:00 Study
11:00-11:30 Revision
1:00-2:00 Lunch break
2:00- 5:00 Study
5:00- 6:00 Break
6:00- 9:00 Study
9:00-10:00 Dinner
10:00- 12:00 Study

Little miss had dark circles formed under her eyes after hours of starring at the books. My hairs had started to fall and I used to have tons of dandruff. But I didn't care about my looks. All I care about was my Grades, Academic validation and my career.

"Once I finish these exams, I'll start doing skin care and hair care. I've been very cruel to myself" I had a talk with myself.

Time waits for no man! I was at the gate of my Board centre, with not just hopes but confidence as well, and a pinch of nervousness. My mom had come to drop me on the scooter. I was carrying the hall ticket, a writing pad, pouch and a water bottle. They wanted each and everything transparent just like my life. Wasn't funny. With all this, I entered the gate showing the hall ticket to the guard who checked the stuff I was carrying. Things were pretty good until I reached the examination hall. I was completely filled with nervousness, my heart was pounding really fast and I started forgetting things. I drank a lot of water. It was exactly 9o'clock and we were given the question papers. I felt a relief. RELIEF?

Yes Relief. It was a relief of knowing the answers. I had studied everything. I started with reading the last question. I knew it. I analyzed the last second question. I knew it as well. Gradually I examined the whole question paper and surprisingly I was able to answer most of the questions. Now it was the time to write.

It took me bloody three hours to finish but somehow I managed to do it. Exactly at 12o'clock they snatched our papers. I was satisfied.

Like REALLY satisfied. I collected the stationary which was messed up. As soon as I left the centre, my eyes were searching for my mom. She was waving from the crowed with excitement and a little bit of anxiousness.
Our eyes met and the first thing she asked was

"How was the paper"
"It went great Ma!! I'm expecting 90 at least."
"OH- That's greatt my BABAY" saying this she showed a relief on her face.

I started studying for the next exam, with no attention on Nishit, Vidhya and blah blah. Finallyyy the exams were finished and I was able to sleep with PEACE. I logged in to the internet and what I saw was tons of messages from Nishit. I ignored them. I still wasn't ready to talk to him.

After a break of some days, I started studying for the entrance tests I had to give for a GOOD college. I had tons of exams in the upcoming month, and I had no time for Boston drama. A week later, I appeared for my first entrance test and it was fucking difficult.

I somehow managed to attend it. It went average but I was happy. Ended up scoring 94%. At least I was satisfied.

My mom expected more but yes I got admission in the college I wanted to study in. I took admission in one of the best college of Mumbai.

FINALLY I was studying psychology professionally. As a main subject!!

I asked my parents to permit me for a solo trip but of course they denied. A girl belonging to a brown middle class family is never supposed to travel alone. So, they took me to a family trip. LONAVALA.

Lol never mind. I am not going to complain. Nishit tried to reach out and I finally answered his call. He had no complains why I wasn't picking up his phone since three months, why I wasn't replying to his texts, Why did I disappeared.

All he asked was how did I do in my exams. I was surprised. I have no words to describe how I felt. But all I can say is I questioned him for being a human.

But afterall why would he even care. He doesn't even give a fuck. Me ghosting him has nothing to do with his life because he doesn't care. I told him how I got admission in one of the best college of Mumbai. And he congratulated me.

I asked him about Vidhya.

"Aarohiii! Vidhya is great! We both bought an apartment and are roommates now."

"YOU GUYS ARE DOING LIVE-IN???" My Indian ass wasn't able to digest it. It was a moment where I was proud of my parents for raising me like this. After all, I own the blood of an average Indian family.

"YEAH- kind of, I mean it's nothing wrong in it." He said.

It was the first time I questioned him for being him. This wasn't Nishit. This isn't the same guy who helped me returning the resistor. The head boy in him had died.

This was all I felt. I somehow managed to end the conversation. I was happy him as well as Vidhya. I realised that Nishit was actually right when he said that I have many people to meet in this world and I haven't even started the journey yet.

A crush is just a lack of information. INDEED. I had completely moved on from him now. Although after his rejection, I used to say that I forgot him already but deep down I knew that I still have feeling for him. And that's how teenage love is, Right? Insane, cheesy and cringe.

I had two months for myself until the college formalities gets filled. I wanted to do something for myself. For the first time. It the very first time I was joining a non-scholastic activity.

I got myself into basketball classes 4 kilometers away from my home. Now, my mom allowed me to drive. Surprising! Even I had a vehical now, like those cool kids had in school. Oppsss, I wasn't in school now. It was very normal for a 12th pass student to drive.

My parents are very strict when it comes to legal matters. They never let me drive, neither they let me sit behind those friends who used to drive without license (Specially BOYS lol.) I need not need to mention that.

I was having fun going to basketball classes every evening. I made a lot of new friends there. We used to warm up during the first fifteen minutes. It was very tiring in the initial days. I was getting out of breathe and produce lots of lactic acid. Hahaha it's the first time I used that term. Finally I'm implementing the science I read in 10th grade.

As an average brown girl I was always told to study and only study. There was no thing called extra curicullem activities at my home. I was sent to tuition classes and was told to study all day except Sundays.

Due to this I had really chubby and had lost my flexibility. I was around five feet and eight inches tall and fifty five kilograms in weight. My mom always used to tell me that she was fifty three kilograms when she got married.

Maybe this was one of a reason why I joined basketball classes, to get fit. I really enjoyed something for the first time in my life. It was the best decision ever. But I had to say goodbye to it someday.

I received an e-mail from the institute; it says that the classes would start from next week. I had to leave Gandhinagar. Finally the time had come.

I started packing my clothes. My mom made homemade laddoos for me and packed some snacks as well. I was sad because I wasn't able to carry much of my clothes due to the hostel protocols. I finally had to repeat clothes like my mom does.

She wears those same standard five pairs of clothes on repeat even though she has a full wardrobe of branded dresses. How boring life gets.

No excitement at all. According to my mom, she finds this activity comfortable.

She says 'Repeating clothes saves the environment and new outfits becomes preserved for some special occasion." INDEED.

Before leaving Gandhinagar, I gave a call to Lilly, telling her that I'm finally living my dreams. But what I saw was a little hard to digest. She declined my call. She never does that.

I ignored this behavior assuming that she must be busy. But alas, she wasn't. She ghosted me. She removed me out of her life.

She blocked me from social media. One more time Miss. Aarohi Mehta was broken.

"Why always with me?" I felt. I had my train to Mumbai in next 5hours. And I didn't know what to do. Why was everybody so changed? Why did I felt a generation gap with the people of MY age? I started doubting myself whether I could help myself settle in Mumbai or not?

My parents were really happy and excited to say goodbye to me. And I didn't want to ruin their excitement.

The hug my mom gave me on the railway station was the most comfortable thing ever. And I had no idea when would I get to hug her tightly once again. I designed a smile on my face and said goodbye to my parents. But only I knew that it was a fake one.

CHAPTER FOUR

Eleven Hours

I had reserved the side birth of train. Just like Kareena Kapoor from 'Jab we met'. I always do that, in a hope to find my 'Adatiya'. But all I got was a lady with her son who was somewhat eight years old. I had a journey of ten hours, And the train was running an hour late. I had nothing to do except over thinking about Lilly.

Why would somebody do that? I would never do that with anybody, and then I recalled that she was the one who advised me to block Nishit. It became explainable now.

I wanna meet myself from another person's point of view and experience my whole energy now, So that I'll at least get to know what was wrong in me which forces everybody to leave. I wanted a break from my own life now. I was genuinely tired now.

The lady saw me zoned out and offered me some *theplas*.

"*Beta, thepla khase*?" she said in a *kathiawadi* accent. I denied, as I was taught not to eat anything offered by strangers. She smiled, and started eating with her son.

I denied but I was hungry, I remembered mom had packed *dhoklas* for dinner. I unboxed it and started having it.

All the railway caterers started their daily chants "*Gujrati, Punjabi, Kathiawadi sab thali milega. Dinner, Lunch,*

Breakfast sab available hai!" On repeat,

It gave me nostalgia to the time we, the grand family along with cousins travelled to *Masoori*. Alas, those days were gone. Now everybody's busy with their university shit.

The *dhoklas* were amazing. I wanted more...

Mumbai was still 6 hours away and it was time to sleep. I always feared missing out the station if I sleep. I didn't sleep completely.

My mind was partially conscious and I was able to understand the announcements.

And, of course, I was still over thinking about Lilly's strange behaviour.

I thought to text her, just wanted the answer of "WHY?" But sometimes, not getting an answer is better than getting one

I started scrolling to distract myself. Thankfully, I had packed my earphones, it was the best time to listen to Taylor Swift.

I started playing illicit affairs, "And you know damn well for you, I would ruin myself A million little times."

Nothing hits you but that one relatable song will make you burst into tears.

The train had finally reached to Mumbai now. It had become a local Metro now. I heard it from my cousin that once a train enters into Mumbai, it becomes a local train and everybody's reservation gets cancelled.

I got off from the train at the Dadar station. It was six in the morning. Mumbai is totally opposite of what I dreamt of.

I realised why it was called the struggling city. It took me an hour to reach the hostel by renting a rikshaw.

I wasn't ready for this. I really wasn't. It was yesterday when I learnt alphabets and now, I'm twelve hours far from my home, In a hostel, where I will have to do everything by myself. I am not ready at all. I miss my mom already.

But there's no come back. It was too late.

CHAPTER FIVE

Struggle

I was at the gate of my hostel. It was a three story red coloured building. The rector madam, her name was Rashmi. She asked me for my admission receipt and other details and showed me the way to my room. I entered my room.

It had two single beds, two metal study tables and an old wooden almira to put your luggage in. The rector said that my roommate will sign in by tomorrow afternoon.

Saying this she left the room and I unpacked the bag and organise my stuff. The room was not at all aesthetic. The most importantly it did not have SUNLIGHT. How mean!!!

I had five days until my college, I decided to give a touch up to my room. I bought some Taylor Swift printouts from the nearest stationary, and some fake leaves to stick on the wall. It somewhat looked good.

I checked my phone and saw three missed calls from Nishit.

"What on earth does he wants now?"

Me: Ooi! You called?

Nishit: yeh, just wanted to wish you for your college life.

Me: Ohh, thanks!

Nishit: I hope you make a great success and find someone

Me: Find someone?

Nishit: Your man of dreams, your boyfriend.

Me: Excuse me, I'm not here to make boyfriends and girlfriends. I'm here to study. And can you please not talk about it?

Nishit: Okay fine...but what happened?

Me: Uhh.. You remember Lilly? She ghosted me. She isn't picking up my calls, she removed me from her friend list, and ain't replying to my texts as well.

Nishit: That's so mean, do you want me to talk to her?

Me: No! I'm fine without her. Maybe she made some other friend there. Her priorities are changed buddy.

Nishit: You sure?

Me: Yes I'm and I gotta now BYE

Saying this, I left my room to have lunch in the mess. I was freaked out. My mom had told me that she somehow consumed the worst kind of food in her hostel.

The 'sabzi' was half cooked, 'daal' was very soupy and the 'roties' are torture to the human kind.

I had my first meal in Dadar girls hostel. It wasn't that bad. Maybe my mom trained me for this day. But yes, the roties were definitely partially raw.

I sat all alone this time. I didn't know whom to be friends with. All the girls were GenZ types.

I'm a genZ as well but, I had generation gap with people of my age. The same day at the dinner, I sat with a group of girls laughing on a lame joke.

They introduced themselves and started laughing on lame jokes. It reminded me of Lilly. I distracted myself. I thought of the times when Lilly and I used to laugh on those girls who think they look cool.

My eyes started secreting tears, somehow stopped them to fall till I reach my room. I silently ate my daal makhni and left for my room asap.

****

Saw a missed call notification on my phone. Mom. I called back. She asked me for the update of my whole day.

"Beta, how's Mumbai? You good with the food? Like your roommates? Hope they're from a good family"

"Ma, Mumbai is amazing, The food is not that bad and my roommates have not arrived yet. Rashmi ma'am, the rector told me that they'll join the room by tomorrow afternoon."

"That's great beta, Study well. We miss you"

"I miss you too mom!"

I layed on the bed staring at the wall. My inner me was speaking. What should I do now? Why am I so unlovable. Everybody leaves me. The guy I loved rejected me and now he is happy with some other girl. My best friend ghosted me out of nowhere. I've nobody now. Nobody to share my problems. Nobody with whom I can share my happiness, achievements, updates. NOBODY.

I kept staring at the wall. Until I realised it was 6 in the morning and I had slept.

"It was a beautiful day, the birds were chirping. The students were working out in the garden and the sun my orange in colour. Beautiful like never before."

Don't expect me to say that. The sun was beautiful, but I had no time to watch it rise more. The birds were definitely chirping. But the metro and the vehicles were chirping louder. And students working out in the garden?? NO, they were standing in a queue for their turn to brush their teeth and bath.

Aarohi Mehta! Welcome to the hostel life! It sucks but is fun when you have friends. I don't have them. It's okay Aarohi, your roommates have not arrived yet. Don't feel left out!

I debated with the mini me.

After waiting for an eternity, It was finally my turn to bath. It generally takes me half an hour to bath including washing my hairs. Adter 15 mins the girls started knocking the doors.

"Madam, this is not your home, Open!!" I didn't know what to reply. How can you knock someone who's in the bathroom, give them some privacy dude! Finally opened the door. The girl standing outside was giving me a death stare. It was weird. I ignored and left.

I thought to discover Dadar. Visited the nearest public park where I bought some icecream and sat on the bench for hours observing the kids, aunties doing their morning yoga. And old aged uncles sitting in a circular group and discussing about their life.

I had my breakfast in the nearest restaurant. I ordered idli and sambhar. Paid the bill and left the shop by 11o'clock.

Reached the hostel by 11:37, my roommates had finally arrived. I was excited to meet them.

***

"Hello, I'm Aarohi Mehta. I'm from Gandhinagar."

"Oh, Hi. I'm Varsha Lyer from Coimbatore, nice to meet you."

"You're from which college? What course are you doing?"

"I'm from St.Xavier, here for the java course. What about you?"

"I'm from the same college, humanities department. I'm doing B.Sc in Neuro psychology. My college will start soon after two days."

"Oh that's cool, I always wanted to know about psychology. Can you read my mind?"

"Varsha, Psychologists cannot read minds! In fact nobody can read your mind!!

"Hahaha I know, I'm just leg pulling"

"Ohh, Do you need help to unpack your luggage?"

"Uh, no It's okay. I'll do it."

Varsha had a south Indian accent. She was brown in colour, had shoulder length hairs and average 5'3 height. She was pretty deep brown eyes and had beautiful face cut.

Till she was unpacking her bag, I sat next to her, On my chair waiting for her to finish unpacking.

"Do you want to roam around the hostel campus? I'll show you"

"That's cool, let's go! But in the evening, I'm really tired and it's 2 in the afternoon, the sun in on the head."

"Sure, Do you want to eat something? Had lunch?"

"Yes, I did while i reached the station. Oh cool!"

CHAPTER SIX

Building Friendship

"Dadar is quiet good, but quiet congested if I say to be honest."

"The only thing to eat here is pavs. Misal pav, Vada pav, Pav bhaji, Chole pav, pav pav. Huhh." said Varsha

"haha pav pav, that was quiet funny. Well, lemme take you to a South Indian Madrasi restaurant."

"REALLY?? Let's go!"

***

"1 masala dosa please and a filter coffee" Varsha ordered her food to the waiter as she continued saying "What would you like to have?"

"Not very much, just a filter coffee"

We talked about out life when we used to live in Gandhinagar and Coimbatore. She told me that she had mastered Bharatnatiyam. And she loves listening to carnatic music. Her mother is a carnatic music singer. And her father is a scientist.

Her story was very typical south Indian type. Very traditional living. Father is a scientist mother is a singer and you do bharatnatiyam.

"Oh, lemme guess, you have a wooden home where there's a well in between and, around the wells, rooms are surrounded in a cubic path."

"HAHAHA HOW DO YOU KNOW??"
"oh my god, was I right???"
"ofc not" she gave me a death stare.
"Oh.. sorryyy, I thought all south Indians live in this kind of home.
"We definitely have this home, it's in my village where my grandparents live."
"See, I told ya!! Hahaa"
We both looked at eachother and laughed.

"So... tell me you gujaratis always eat *dhokla, thepla, khaman, jalebi fafda* and all"

"Welll, don't know about others but my mom makes thepla every other day and when I was coming here she packed me a tiffin filled with *dhoklas*."

We were breaking eachother's cultural stereotypes. It was fun. We took a walk in the Abhilasha Public Park. It was almost seven in the evening. We returned back to the hostel.

We had nothing to do now, the hostel didn't even have a television to do time pass. Varsha and I watched Chennai Express on her laptop at night after a not so bad dinner.

"It's one of my all time favourite movie"
"I'm watching this for the seventh time now" varsha replied
Both of us started vibing to the lyrics.

Beat pe lagade tu thumka,
One two three four, get on the dance floor

"Hahahahhahhahhha it was fun! Wanna dance more?"

"Yes ofcorse, lemme put the flop song. C'MON MAKE SOME NOISE.!!"

Distance moonu moonu
Moonu colouru whiteu

Nightu background whitu whitu
Nightu colouru blacku
Why this kolavari kolavari kolavari di!

"OMGGG!! Your're such a fun person Aarohi! I've never danced like this before"

"Hahaha this is just a trailer, *picture to abhi baki hai mere dost!!*

"Chalo let's sleep, We'll go for window shopping tomorrow in the Bombay market followed by juhu beach"

***

"Juhu is very crowded. Mumbai is sweaty. I miss Coimbatore, cool, chilled and a lil bit hot."

"I thought south India is always hot, regardless the seasons."

"no dumb, it's not like that"

"Oh.. Wanna have some Vadapav?"

"Sure!! It must be spicy; I've never tried maharastrian food."

CHAPTER SEVEN

First Day

Finally, it's that day!! The first day of my college! We have grown up!! I won't be wearing uniform now! I won't have to apply oil in my hairs and tie up two choties!

I woke up with full excitement. I washed my hairs, dried them in the pankha. And selected a pair of baggy jeans and a full sleeve white coloured tees with brown strips on it.
I tied my hair into a pony tail and left for college with a small bag which carried two notebooks and a laptop.

I was at the gate of my college. It was a huge building with never ending campus. Some students were playing basketball, some were cycling and some were sitting around a tall handsome guy playing guitar.

Everything felt like Karan Johar's movie.

I stepped ahead to the notice board to check my class no. Where a bunch of girls and boys came to me, they were my seniors. It was too late but I finally realised that I was being ragged!!

OMG I was being ragged!! I'm in a college now!

"Fresher?" A not so tall, average looking guy asked from the gang.

"yes!"

"We're your seniors, sing a song for us?"

"Are you sure? Cuz I'm a great singer. If I will sing you'll force yourself to keep quiet.

"*Abe Oooo shani banti hai*" A tall zero figured girl in a crop top, shorts and a lether jacket said in a Marathi accent

I started singing without giving any explanation.

Sujalam Suphalam
Malayaja shitalam
Shasyashyamalam Mataram
Vande Mataram!

"OMG Gurll!! You're awesome!!" Everyone near me clapped as I finished singing. All those seniors went speechless they shook my hands and left without saying a single word.

I felt proud of myself after a very long time. I searched for my class and sat on the on the corner without interacting with anybody.

I missed my schoolmates, I missed Nishit, I missed Lilly. I wondered what she must be doing right now! And Nishit? Should I text him or not I was fighting with my urge to control itself. I wanted to tell someone about what happed in ragging and how smart I am. I finally texted Nishit.

"HEY! What's up"

Kept my phone aside as the lecturer entered! Mr.Govind. teaches us statistics. After an hour, I checked my phone.

"Hello Aarohi! What's up!
"Nvm.. First day at college. Killed the ragger kid's self esteem"

"Yahooo that's like my gurl"

Did he just call me his girl?? Did he just forget that he has a girlfriend? Both of them are doing live in from past one year!! And here he is calling me HIS girl!

Aarohi, you need to calm down! Stop being ridiculous

***

College Canteen

"Varsha!! How was your day? I'm really tired. Long day at school."

"College."

"oppss!! Hahahahaha"

"Let's order something,Sandwiches?"

" Cheese grilled for me"

So tell me Aarohi, do you have a boyfriend?"

"....boyfriend.. uh.. no yaar koi mila hi nai!"

" Whatt! how's that possible koi mila nai. You're so pretty I don't believe"

"Omg thankss but I'm single what about you?"

"I had a boyfriend in 10th class. Then he dumped me during the final exams. He came back to me after results but I broke up. Because why not?"

"hahha acceptable."

"Accha listen I'll take a leave now. I have a lecture in 10. Will directly meet you at room now. Do you want me to pack lunch for you if you're going to be late?"

"It's okay darling. I'll meet you in the mess at 1:30. See you"

***

Hostel mess

"Varsha..... UHH...*nothing*"

"What?"

"There was a guy.... We're friends. I had a crush on him in 10th class and I confessed. He rejected me but we were still good friends. After two years. Turns out that he has a girlfriend in London and they're living together.

I had a small talk with him and you know what he said?...."

"what?"

"He called me HIS girl. I'm not day dreaming of me ending up with him. I just want to know whyy!!!"

".... Aarohi Mehta pay attention. Just because he called you his girl doesn't mean that he literally meant that.. You're just over thinking..

Maybe he said that unintentionally. Boys are dumb. They don't know half of the things they're talking about."

"Yeahh.. maybe."

CHAPTER EIGHT

Fresher's Party

College was fun. We were invited to the fresher's party. It's an event organised by seniors to welcome new students to a college or university. You meet your seniors. I was in a hope to find a nice guy. I was extremely excited. I had already decided what to wear. My mom approved that dress as well.

My heart was pounding with joy. Anticipation had filled me I was eager for what was going to come.

I was waiting for this since 4th grade.

The saree I wore was blue in colour with small floral patterns. I wore a decent pearl pendent and had tied up my hairs in pony tail.

I was not at all fashionable. I had no collection of foot wears.

My parents never let me wear fancy footwear. They believed that pencil heels damages your lower back. That is why, all I wore with my saree was white sneakers.

The hall was full of crowd. I had no idea what to do. Everybody was dancing with their boyfriends and girlfriends. Some were around the stage and some were in groups gossiping. I searched for my classmates.

Seems like they haven't arrived yet. I was missing Lilly. Wondering what kind of life she must be living. I wanted to update her each and everything.

I was standing on the corner with a glass of coke and watching others dance. A guy came to me. I had seen him before. In that crowded room, A handsome unknown guy was walking towards me. Mystery surrounds him. His eyes, like oceans, Deep and enchanting. He was drawing closure to me. He was charming and confident. His dark hair were perfect yet messy, and his athletic build was evident even under his casual clothes.

I wonder who he is. What stories lies within him. I felt like he was the book left unread. It suddenly popped up in my mind. He was the Guitar guy!!

"Hello lady! I'm Agastya Bapat."

"Hi, I'm Aarohi Mehta."

"Would you like to dance?"

"Umm.. I'm afraid and I'm good in here"

"Ohh, Nice sarree by the way. Suits you"

It was the second time a guy had praised me after Nishit.

"Oh, c'mon it's not that good" I meant to say praise me more.. Is it that difficult to understand girls.

"No I mean it. It suits you really well. Infact you look the prettiest here"

Oh shitttt, I can sense this going somewhere else.

"uhh.. enough.. Don't try me out."

"But that's what you wanted right? HAHAHA"

"You can read minds?"

"Lol no. But that's what girls generally want to hear when they pretend to deny a compliment."

"OMG. That's so true. I feel embarrassed!"

"No need to be. It's okay. And it's normal"

"So... Comfortable dancing with me now?" He asked as soon as the DJ shifted the romantic song to *Kal ho na ho's* it's the time to disco. I was impressed. I replied in affirmative.

After a few sets of couple of minutes. The Dj shifted back to romantics. I did not mind leaving the dance floor. It was dark but good enough to see eachother's face. He asked me through his sparkling eyes for my permission.
I approved.
We danced to *Janam Janam* like professional dancers.I had never felt like this with Nishit.

"You're a great dancer Aarohi Mehta."

"No nothing like that. I suck at dancing. I'm myself wondering how I rocked it."

"Haha it was very gradeful. We had great chemistry"

"Are you flirting"

"oh shitt, you caught me." He giggled saying that.

"So that's why you were playing guitar in the campus. To impress girls??" That was an indirect way to ask about his girlfriend

"Omg NOO. I had no intentions to do that."
"Hahah I'm just pulling your legs."
"By the way.. what you doing?"

"I'm doing B.Sc Psychology. What about you?

"Ohh.. I'm from the medical department.
Currently doing MBBS. Later on planning to do M.D and then Neurosurgery."

"Ohhh I'm going for Neuropsychology.

We'll be hand in hand. That's soo much of studying. And hellow Mr. Bapat. What are you doing in our fresher's party then?"

" Sounds interesting to work with you in future.

My friend invited me. I wasn't crashing the party. HELLO!

"haha.. Even if you were. It's none of my loss."

"So.. dinner?"

"Yeah.. have it.. Have it."

"Very funny… Bye"

"Agastya waittt… I was kidding. Let's have it together."

"Salad?" he asked

"Ummm NO.. I will directly have the starters and the main course. Salads are not worth it. Demands space in the stomach as well as in the plate…"

'HAAH.. nice theory."

After a heavy satisfying dinner, I thought to sign off. Others were still performing. I gave Agastya a tiring face.

"Are you tired? It's 9:30 already. Should I drop you?"

"It's okay. I'll book a cab."

"Please. I insist Aarohi"

"Fine" Agastya seemed a nice guy. I couldn't deny him.
"Of course he is a nice Guy.!"

He dropped me to the hostel on his bike.

"Thankyouu… But it was no need to drop."

"It's 9:30.. Not safe to go through a cab, the location was quite distant. That's why. "

"Well. Thanks"

"Aarohi, Can I get your number?"

"WHY?"

"nevermind"

"Wait.. give me your phone!"

***

I was pretending to sleep. But all I could do was recall what happened in the party.

How he respectfully asked me for my concern to put his hand on my waist. I've never been so close to a guy. Whoever will marry this guy is definitely very lucky. Or maybe I'm very lucky. UHHH.. That's just my brain planning my whole life for no reason. But this time, my intuitions were giving me signs as well. Or maybe I'm was thinking.

He drew me with his vibrant energy and infectious laugh. He mustered up the courage to approach me to me ask me out for dance. As I danced with him I felt an undeniable spark, and he knew that I wanted to explore this connection further. Little did he know that this chance encounter would lead to a journey of love, laughter, and adventure with a girl who captured his heart.

CHAPTER NINE

Love?

Agastya took my number but we had never talked or met eachother after the fresher's party. Maybe he forgot me. He never texted neither did he call. I was busy completing my syllabus for the semester.
I had tons of pending assignments I had to complete. I had no time to hangout. I still had a little hope to meet him and dance with him. But I did not entertain it much.

I had my semester exams in fifteen days. Varsha and I were barely meeting. We came to our rooms just to sleep. I was sitting in the university library the whole day.

It demands several hours to find the reference books.

I had my practicals next week. I had to find a subject. Varsha was a great subject for my practicals. We even had to organise a psychology fest by the end of the month.

I was given to design the posters and banners.

I was going through lack of sleep, I had fifty shades of dark circles and I had to get a haircut.

Having to complete all these duties, I was still daydreaming about whom?

"Agastya Bapat."
    Yes darling!
    I was so in love with him. Was it love at first sight?

NO, I don't believe in it. But, in the silence of night I think of him. His presence is a balm to my weary soul. A gentle touch of him had soothed my troubled mind. I really cherish the moments we had spent together.

His touch, it had care, concern and respect.

It brought shivers down my spine.

"AWWWWWWWWWW!! IS THIS WHAT LOVE FEELS LIKE?"

Love is believed to be beautiful. Nobody knows what it feels like to be in love. It's a mixed feeling.

Sometimes it feels like a warm embrace. It feels like a comforting presence in every space. Love is patient, Love is kind.

It's a treasure that is hard to find. It feels like a soothing rain baby. Love can also be tragic.

If it makes you smile then it can also make you cry. Love makes you hope against hope for a happy ending.

"WoW.! This is beautifull. Did you meet Agastya after that?"

Yes I did. My hopes were almost died. I had almost forgotten him by the end of the semester. I was done with my practicals and theories. When I got a text from Mr.Bapat.

"Hello Aarohi, It's my birthday next week. Would you like hanging out?"

"Who else is coming?"

"You, Me, the friend I told you about and his girlfriend"

"That would be really awkward for you all. You guys enjoy. I'm out. I've got work to do for the upcoming psychology fest."

"It would be great if you would've come. Your presence will be missed. LOL"

"Shut up dumb heheehe"

"Why did you reject the invitation??"

Because I had work to do. I cannot put my work on second priority. You wanna know what happend next?

On Agastya's Birthday I wished him. He asked me whether he could join the psychology fest and then we could go out for dinner. Just two of us.

I hesitated. I defunately denied for the dinner think but the vadpav we had together was the best.

I don't love him. I believed. But, as soon as we decided to meet the next moment I made a very important call. My parlour aunty. I booked an appointment for a haircut and waxing.

***

Oouch It hurts. !! The lady's hands were very brutal. Seems like she had a fight with her husband.

"OOUCH... SHHH .. OUCHH SLOWLY..."

"It's done.. What kind of haircut do you want?"

"I want to trim my hairs. Remove the split ends, and cut the bangs shorter.. Don't make it very short.

I like my hairs long. Just remove the damaged ones"

"Alright.... I need to cut around 5-6cm"

NOOO that's too short..

"Madam I need to. They're all damaged. It's okay they'll grow back in few months."

***

Psychology fest

"Aarohi, you look lovely! I see you've got a new haircut. It really suits you"

"Aww, thank you for noticing! I was worried it might be too short"

"Not at all, it's perfect. You look stunning with this cut. I must say, it's exactl how I envisioned it"

"Haha, what do you mean by 'exactly how you envisioned'? That sounds like something my mom would say" I continued "I'll have to run, I have a presentation in 10 minutes. And I'd love if you could attend"

"Ofcourse I'll. I wouldn't miss it for the world"

***

Ladies and Gentlemen. Now I would like to call Miss.Aarohi Mehta, the wise captain of Woman empowerment and mental health awareness for a mesmerising message. Over to you Aarohi.

Hello to everybody present here.
Sorry guys, I'm a very awkward public speaker HAHA

So tell me, What does it mean to be an empowered woman in today's world? DRAUPADI.

A woman whose fate was ticked at a game of dice. Who was dragged into a court while menstruating and disrobed in the presence of her own husband's family and the strongest and wisest men known to history.

She was helpless the epic goes to say until Lord Krishna came to rescue her.

But do we still have the luxury of having Lord Krishna?

The women of the world have relied far too long on a bystander to come and save them.

So is the message here to wait for Krishna or to become your own Krishna?

An empowered Woman doesn't want special reservations. What they want is equal access to opportunities for Men and Women. We do not want equality. We want equal Importance.

People out there think that if a woman is earning in lakhs she's not capable of becoming a wife or raise kids. People think that if she is a housewife, a wife material.. completly dedicated in her kids then she cannot go out and earn?

Why are women given choices? Either this or that? Can't we have both?

Giving them choices is like telling a lioness to stay in the cave all the time and raise the kids. Only the lion will go out and bring food for them. This is highly unfair. Women don't want this guyzzz wake up!

Hope I did not bore you..

Signing off

Aarohi Mehta

"Heyy dumb.. Are you mad or whattt? Hope you did not bore us? Gurll you rocked it!!*Paagall*"

" OMG thank you so much Agastya. You scared me. I thought it wasn't good."

"You delivered it. It has to be good. Like, shut the fuck up."

Is he trying me out? Or just praising. Whatever it was. Feels so comforting. He gives me butterflies.

"I've to be present her for an hour more. Then we'll go somewhere for dinner. Okay?"

"As you say madam!"

***

"Wanna have some Chinese, I'll take you to the best place in Dadar" He offered as we started walking to find a rickshaw

"Actually, No. Let's go for a Vadapav date."

"DATE...???"

He came closer to me. Our fingers intertwined, sending a spark of elasticity through me. I made no effort to pull away, entranced by the warmth of his touch.

He began to speak his, his words faltered, "N-no, I meant to say...." But before he could finish, he leaned in, his lips brushing against my forehead in a soft, gentle kiss.

The tender gesture was so unexpectedly old-fashioned that I couldn't help but be charmed. And in that moment I realised that I was falling deeply in love with him.

My heart skipped a bead when Agastya's hands enveloped mine, his grip warm and reassuring. We walked in comfortable silence, the only sound being the gentle rustling of leaves beneath our feet. Finally I found my voice and my words barely above a whisper.

"A-Agastya... I love you"

His face lit up with a radiant smile. "I love you too. Aarohi, I've been waiting to share something with you for so long"

My curiosity was piqued "What is it?"

His eyes sparkled with excitement. "A poem I wrote about my future wife"

My mind raced. Does he see me as his future wife? Is this moving too fast? But the feeling in my heart told me otherwise. It felt right.

"I'd love to hear it" I said, in a voice filled with anticipation.

As we stood there, hands still clasped, Agastya began to recite his poem, his words weaving a spell of love longing around my heart.

I hide you from the world,
in my music, poetry and my art
In a room full of people,
My heart would think about you
In your eyes, I'd see stars above.
In your smile the warmth of love, I feel your presence close to mine, As we dance together in the refrigerator light.
You pop up like a gentle breeze,
That soothes my soul and sets me free With every breath, every sigh, You make my heart feel alive.

I think of you,
Every minute, every second and every breathe of mine
I promised myself to never fall in love until your heart finds
mine.
You are my star,
Whom I adore from afar No matter where ever you are
Our dreams never gonna tarnish and Our love never gonna
vanish
Love,
Your Future Husband

"A...Agastya.. WHATTT OH MY GODD. This is beautiful. I love you sooo much. I lovee you."

"Cheers to the vadapav who's third wheeling right now"

"You're so funnyyy. *Kafi cute.*"

"*Aapki tarah*"

"Ahh, this is ridiculous"

CHAPTER TEN

Our thing

"WHAT!" Varsha reacted as I told her about Agastya."

"Yess. I met him at the fresher's party. His friend invited him"

"Are you sure he's a nice guy. I hope you know everything about him."

"Yes I do. But I don't know whether I'm doing it right or not. Because you know firstly, I'm in the 1ˢᵗ year of college. Soon to be 2ⁿᵈ . And secondly, I'm completely new to this city."

"I get it. Are you sure he feels the same about you. Go ask him out. And listen. This relationship shouldn't affect your career. For now your first priority is your degree."

"I'm glad to have a friend like you Varsha."

***

"hey Ags! Wanna meet yoy at 6a.m at Agora hills.this Sunday."

"sure Miss.Mehta Can't wait to see you again"

"bring your guitar as well"

"OKieee"

Agora hills

"This is one of my favourite place in Mumbai. You find calmness in this chaotic fast life of the city.

This place has peace, comfort, nature and now you and your guitar as well." He blushed so hard.

Both of us became silent. Until he started to play my favourite gujarati song from behind.

Ke tane jata joi panghat ni vaate
Maru m,an mohi gayu
Ke tara rupala gora gora ghate
Maru man mohi gayu

He tried his best to sing in gujarati accent. But I loved that hidden *Marathi-ness*.

"Aaru, this one was for you"
"I love you Agastya. I love you so muchhh"
"I love you too Aarohi"
"When did you realise that you love me Ags"
"Ahhh.. Damn I was waiting since forever to answer to this question. Remember you talked about equal importance and not equality during the psychology fest.

You talked how a woman can do corporate and be a family star as well.

I'm not a feminist. I'm a humanist. I believe in equal opportunity and importance to both woman and man. That was the time I realised I love you and you're the one"
"Ohh.. and?"

"And you're the best thing that has ever happened to me. I feel so blessed to be able to meet you. You know what, It's a quote.

It's ordinary to love the beautiful but it's beautiful to love the ordinary. And you the what's the most beautiful thing?"

"What Ags?"

*"To be the ordinary,*To maintain simplicity. Aarohi I've never met a girl like you who's so simple yet the most beautiful. Your personality litrally shouts out that beauty lies in simplicity. I hope I impressed you"

"You don't need to impress me. I'm already impressed by you.

And stop Over exaggerating. I cannot digest compliments."

"No, I need to. Afterall that's what women want. They want to be praised, loved and feel special. Women are very simple.

Also, I'm not over exaggerating. This is the most precious thing about you. #simplicity"

"Ags, how many times are you going to win my heart?"

"Every single day Aaru. "

"I hope you're not going to break up with me"

"Of course I'm not. It's like you complete me"

"I've started to like cheesy lines."

"I'm proud of you Miss. Mehta. Meet you until next time."

"Hope you're not going to double date"

"Let's see.. surely if I find someone better than you"

"MR. AGASTYA BAPAT!! Don't you dare!"

"Damnn! I'm sorry but you've got a hot death stare and killing eyes" he winked as soon as he said killing eyes.

I couldn't stop giggling.

"See you next soon.."

"Can't wait already"

He came closer to me as he appealed for a warm request. "Lemme wrap you in snug warm hug Ags"

The sun raised as our soul entwined like a gentle tug. Our hands wrapped around, holding tight in the quiet moment of love's pure sunlight.

"Ags.. You know what this felt like?"

It felt like I found my peace, a sense of safety,
a world to cease from the din and chaos,
I escaped into the quiet refuge of our loving space."

"You're impossible Aaru.. the way you describe things has my. Wanna have breakfast? It's 7:30. It's going to take an hour to reach down on the main road."

"lemme take you to my favourite *Misal pav* shop"

"Ohh Miss. Mehta's treat.. impressed"

***

"So tell me Mr. Bapat, Do you have any ex?" I asked curiously with a pinch of possessiveness."

"Will you break up with me if I say *yes* ?"

I hesitated a little.. I don't like to date the person who has exes.. It means that he loved a girl immensely and suddenly out of nowhere his priorities changed.

I would never like to date a guy who loved someone else before. Call me a red flag or whatever. I took so long to answer his question.

"hellow! Aaru??"

"Noo of course not I mean.. Whom did you date before me?"

He made teasing look and giggled "Look at your face. I'm just pulling your leg. I'm a One Woman man"

"You kidding me?? Bitch you scared the fuck out of mr I hate you"

"I love you too."

CHAPTER ELEVEN

Third Person

3 YEARS LATER

Spending time with Agastya was my absolute delight. Being in love felt heavenly, and I never knew it could be this way until I met him. All my problems seem to fade away when we were together.

My past experience with Nishit paled in comparison. I realised why my mom never believed in teenage love- it was fleeting and immature. I had been infatuated with Nishit, but discovering his

live-in-relationship was a wakeup call.

Now, I prayed for Agastya and me to have a love that would stand the test of time, *'Dear God, make our love old enough to last forever and modern enough to survive the times'*.

As I sat in the hostel lobby, enjoying the unseasonal rain, I couldn't wait to finish my final semester exams and meet Agastya. 'How romantic is the *bin mausaam barsaat'* I thought to myself feeling dreamy. But then I snapped back to reality rembering the harsh truth- it was global warming.

A text popped up on the screen of my phone.

I ignored it. It rang again. Ignored. One more time. And once again.

I finally checked it out of curiosity. I was confident that Ags must have planned a date for us. It was .. . "Hello Aarohi, hope you're good I'm extremely sorry for rejecting you that day. It's like one doesn't value the pure water unless you are given toxic water to drink......"

This is what I could read through the notifications.

My immediate reaction after reading that was "WHATTT!"

I wanted to know what he meant. "Nishit can you please explain what do you mean?

"I broke up with Vidhya.. I made her leave my apartment. She's back in PG."

"And?" I replied as if I don't care.. *I actually don't* .

"And I'm really sorry for rejecting you. I've always loved you but something stooped me from accepting your proposal. But here I'm completely confident about my decision.

I love you Aarohi. I love you so much since we met."

WHAT THE FUCK.. *SINCE WE MET*? What a liar. Boys can lie about anything to impress a girl.

"Sorry bro.. Too late. First of all you 'removed' Vidhya as if she's a trash. And now when you're all alone you're expecting me to be your girlfriend.

And what is this I loved you since the day we met. STOP LYING."

"I'm not lying baby.. Please give me a chance."

"DON'T BABY ME! I'm happy with my life. It's been three years of me being in a relationship with a guy. You've given me enough breakdowns."

"Can we meet? I'm coming to India next week. Where are you?"

"None of your business"

He did not reply to it. I immediately called Agastya. He didn't pick up. I texted him '*call me back asap*'. It was almost three years of us together .

Now we didn't have any late night romantic chats. All we chatted was about university stress, budget of our dates and amount of money we paid for eachother. My mom was right. It's only fun in the beginning.

Agastya called me after bloody eleven hours. "What happened Aaru."

"Is this your as soon as possible?? You called me after eleven hours.

What if I was being kidnapped?"

"WoW!!! Imagine you being kidnapped and texting me '*call me asap*'. Babes I was busy with the opds. And firstly, who's going to kidnap you. Look at your face. You can scare anybody"

"WHatttt Agas can you stop roasting me. I'm your girlfriend!!"

"Is it written in our constitution that boyfriends cannot roast girlfriends?"

"Agastya I'm mad at you!!

He kept silent for a couple of seconds "………again or still?"

Agastya Bapat should be given a noble price to make a mad girlfriend blush so hard. "Aww……."

"Can't meet you this Sunday. I'll check on you tomorrow whenever I'm free. Will wait in the canteen.

"sure Ags. I want to tell you something really important."

"sure.. Cya tomorrow. Luv you."

***

It was a perfect day. Cloudy weather with a pinch of showers. Cool, not so humid and a beautiful start of morning. I wore a pair of comfortable red pants, a plain black tunic and a red stole with my hairs tied up in a pony tail. I was all set to leave for college.

I was now in the first year of Masters. I had officially elected neuropsychology now.

Just how fast the night changes. I had applied for internship form as well. Saturdays were the most hectic day of the week. I finally got some time and sat in the canteen.

"I'll be there in some time" said the notification from *Agastya.*

Saw a guy coming towards me. I wasn't able to recognise him. He was in a black full sleeved tee, blue denim jeans and goggles on his face. He had a pale ivory skin colour and light brown eyes.

"WHAT THE BLOODY FUCK! NISHIT SHAH!"

"surprise!!"

"Shut up! How did you find my college?"

"Your friend had tagged you on facebook."

"What do you want?"

"you." He slowly got onto his knees and took out a small red box from his pocket. It was a *diamond ring.*

"Nishit don't create a nuisance here. I'm not going to accept."

"*Dear Aarohi,*

In the moment of vulnerability and love. The question hangs in the air. Three simple words filled with hope and fear.

This ring glistening in the light. Symbolising a commitment of forever. The world is standing still. Anticipation has filled the room.

I don't have any expectations or demands. Just a pure and honest plea I have. Will you take this journey with me? And become my partner in life's symphony.

The answer is still unknown but the question I asked is with full sincerity. Will you marry me Miss. Aarohi Mehta?"

"WHAT THE FUCK!" A voice roared up from the crowd.

The man finally managed to come in front to see what's exactly happening.

"AGASTYA!!!" I ran towards him and game him a tight hug.

"It's okay." He whispered in my ears. Nishit stood up on his feet as soon as I ran hugged Ags.

"Hello gentleman. I must say you prepared very well but unfortunately I topped this exam. Please leave her alone. She's my girl." said Agastya in a polite respectful tone.

"I know her since 10th grade." Nishit spoke in a rebellious voice

"And?"

"I can understand her better than you. She's in love with me."

"What a jokee HAHAHHA. Aarohi! I'll drop you to the hostel. Let's go."

CHAPTER TWELVE

Transperancy

Every relationship has conflicts. If love feels heavenly it can also feel like hell.

Agastya did not drop me to the college. Instead he took me to his place. I greeted his mother and went upstairs with him. His mother has always been very sweet to me.

She knew that we're officially in a relationship. And both of us shared a great bond.

Agastya's father was a business man. They had their own companies.

Nishit chose to become a Neurosurgeon rather than handling his father's business.

I entered his room. It was bright. The bright sunlight entered my eyes. It made me uncomfortable. Agastya closed the windows and drew the curtains. Better.

He sat on the edge of his bed and made a serious stare. I brought a bowl chair from the corner of the room and sat right in front of him.

"You can shout at me if you want." I said

" Aaru.. It's been 3 years since we know eachother. You never told me about this guy. Is he your ex? Did you ask him out? Why was he proposing you? And look at his audacity he's saying he knows you better than me!!" He took a pause and continued

"What the fuck Aarohi.. I told you every single thing about my life. Introduced you to my parents as well.!"

"Nishit, Lilly and I were a group of three. He was the headboy of the school. At some point I liked him. I liked him a lot. Lilly encouraged me to ask him out and I did. He rejected. He said you've a long way and you'll meet a lot of people. If I still like him after a decade he's ready to think about me."

"WOW He's a nice guy. I though he must be a bastard."

"HE IS. Few years ago he told me that he made his girlfriend moved on to his apartment in London. That was the time when I finally realised the reality check."

"DAMN! Then why is he daring to marry you now?"

"Because he recently broke up with his girlfriend Vidhya and now he wants someone in replacement of her. And of course I'm the most eligible candidate for that post."

" Dudeee! That's so........So.....l don't even have words to describe."

"He was never like this in his school days. God knows what happened to him after we stopped talking"

"And how's Lilly? Still in contact with her?"

"No. She ghosted me. Reason is still unknown.

She's in Delhi I guess. She had blocked me from all the social media pages as well. And honestly I don't care now."

"Oh god.. It's okay my girl. I'm always there by your side and would never leave you alone." He stood up from the bed and gave a tight hug to me.

"That's what I needed the most right now"

"I know baby. Forget everybody. I'm here. Always. Whenever you need me."

"Nishit was right. I've a long journey to go through. I'm glad that I finally found my mystery man."

"Do you thing I should inform my parents about us?" I asked as he released his arms."

"Of course you should!! Just go for it. I'm okay even if you want some time. We will face them together." He passed a gentle smile to me.

I was all there sitting on his lap. I constantly made sure that I'm not putting stress on his legs. But he seemed to be alright.

"Okay then.. Next Friday! Let us all go to Gandhinagar. You, me, Uncle and Aunty!

"That's like my girl!"

We high-fived eachother and I gave a gentle kiss on his nose resting my hands on his shoulders.

CHAPTER THIRTEEN

Scrutiny

Agastya and I have been thinking of ways to make our relationship official for weeks. We wanted to surprise my parents and disclose in a special way. So he came up with a plan.

"Mom, Dad. I need your help with something" Agastya said to his parents one evening

"What is it, beta? His mother asked, curious

"I want to surprise Aarohi's parents and tell them about our relationship. I was thinking we could all go to Gandhinagar together to meet them.

His parents exchanged a knowing glance. They had been waiting for this moment.

"That's a great idea beta" his father exclaimed. "We're with you all the way."

And so, we made plans to visit Gandhinagar the following weekend. Agastya couldn't wait to see the look on my parent's faces when they found out about our relationship.

As we pulled up to my childhood home, Agastya could feel his nerves fluttering. I took his hand, giving it a reasoning squeeze. "Don't worry, they'll love you", I said with a smile.

My parents, were first surprised to know who was he but they responded very calmly. They were warm and kind, asking him questions about his family, his studies, and his future plans.

Agastya felt at ease, sharing his passion about neuroscience and future plans.

Meanwhile, mom and agastya's parents had a great chatting time. She told my mom that she was a retired teacher and agastya's dad was a businessman.

Agastya was charmed by my parents who showed him my childhood photos and shared stories about my childhood.

As we drove back to Mumbai, we turned eachother with a smile. "I think our parents are going to get along just fine" his eyes twinkling with happiness.

I laughed, snuggling closer to Agastya. "I think you're right" I replied. "Our families are going to love eachother almost as much as we love eachother."

I stayed at Agastya's place that night. Of course, I sneaked in; His parents were unaware about this plan.

We had endless talks in the balcony where we laid a mattress. We talked and stared eachother under the twinkling stars. I wanted more than just looks and stupid endless flirting. I wanted to taste his lips and his neck and his cheeks and everything. I wanted to run my hand through his hair and feel the electricity of love rush through me as I have read in all of the books in my life. I wanted to pull him kin and never let him go.

He leaned in, carefully. Breathing and not breathing and both of our hearts beating between us. He was so close. He was so close that I couldn't feel my legs anymore. I couldn't feel my finger or the cold breeze of monsoon. All I felt was him. Everywhere. As he finally kisses me.

His lips were softer than anything I've ever known. Soft like a first snowfall, like biting into cotton candy, like melting and floating and being weightless in water. It was so effortlessly sweet. He tightened his hands around my waist and ran one up my back pressing me harder against his chest and my hands were in his hairs.

"okay stop this is getting embarrassing now" I laughed attempting to cover his face with my palm.

"This isn't even close to embarrassing." Do you want embarrassment?"

I gasp as he stands up holding me against him and shifting so my legs wrap around his waist. He spins me around until I giggle and cling to him for my dear life. He then kisses my forehead and cheeks and neck as we spin and spin and spin, and he repeated "I love you" over and over.

"Okay stopp put me down!" He falls flat on the mattress and I land on top of him. He's still smiling. The longest smile I've ever seen from him.

"You're dangerous!! I could have fall!"

"You think I'll let you?

CHAPTER FOURTEEN

Graduation

5 Months later

Things were getting tough.. I was already in the second semester. Agastya and I couldn't meet eachother frequently due to his OPDs and finals. After all, he was almost a doctor now. I couldn't wait to hear his name being announced in the topper's list. I couldn't imagine my happiness when I would see him on the stage delivering a speech of gratitude. Is this the same fifteen year old girl who was dumb hopeless about her mystery man? Yes welcome to the reality check. I had to attend Ags's convocation this Saturday.

15th March Saturday

"Mr.Bapat, So how do you feel, in this Academic regalia?"

"I feel....very exciteddddd, merry, loved, and successful with a pinch of nervousness."

"Hahaha You is the man of the match! Go rock it"

After an hour Ags was finally on the floor. Delivering his experience of 'I finally did it' moment.

'Hello ladies and gentlemen. I feel very honoured right now. I've never been on stage before. Okay so I would firstly like to credit my parents, teachers and the love of my life.Aarohi Mehta.'

Oh shittt. I need to stop blushing. I wanna hide my face.

'Lastly, I would obviously give some credits to myself as well. HAHAHAHA. Okay so coming to the point. From being a junior in this college to finally a graduated senior I unlocked a lot of memories. I even sometimes felt like quitting but then I imagined myself in the white coat. Medical school is not a place for smart people guys. It's for those who are crazy enough to want the sense of purpose that fuels their veins. The secret of me standing here right now is. ROMANTICISM. We often misunderstand romanticism with only love. Romanticism is literally what kept me alive during the tough days of M.B.B.S. It's all about glorifying simple acts of everything that exists. I manifested. I never chase this degree. The degree was attracted towards me. <u>The universe works for me and with me.</u> These lines are the secret of my success. Believe me or not. That's what Aarohi taught me. To romanticise, manifest and get back to work'

"DUMBB! Are you mad or what? At least give a hint before mentioning me. I've never felt so awkward"

"So you're telling me you did not have butterflies in stomach when I mentioned your name"

"No"

"Not even when I called you the love of my life"

"No"

"Not even when I'm so close to you, holding you closer, closer and even more close to me' He pulled me towards him with gentle tickling fingers on your waist"

"Okay fine.. I do and I hate you"

"I love you too"

That was the first time when Agastya and I disclosed our relationship and attended an event as official couple. That was the coolest thing ever.

"So... young couples.. We'll leave for home now..." said Ags's mom as she offered me an invitation to have dinner at their place.

I resisted but brown parents, somehow managed to convince me. She's super sweet. And not gonna lie I love her more than Agastya. Her partial silver hair, she had eyes similar to stars with gentle light. Whatever and whenever she spoke was prudent and wise.

But what I saw at Ags's place was unexpected. Aunty told me to cook dinner for everybody. Was that a fucking test???

"*Beta,* I want to eat food cooked by you." Shittt was she showing a brown mother in-law behaviour????

"Aa..*aunty* I'm not a good cook."

"I don't know anything; I want the dinner cooked by both of you in half an hour"

"Agastya as well??"

"Why not???? You both have to spend rest of your life together. I don't want to excuses?"

"FINE MA!!" Agastya whispered being an obedient cutie patotie.

In the kitchen

"Agastyaaaaa!! *Kya karna he???* "

"Chill chill calm down. Wanna make sandwiches?"

"SURE!"

Cooking together was more like having romantic scenes. Dancing around the refrigerator light in slow motion. I see us getting married in my mind, cuddling on the couch, waking up to good morning breakfast cooking together and arguing for no reason. After an hour, we finally somehow managed to make out. And the kitchen looked like a winded vegetable market.

"Presenting veg. grilled cheese sandwiches by chef #Aarastya!! Make a loud round of applause!!"

"Kudos to you Aarastya! Looks delicious let's see how it tastes." Said *aunty* as she tasted a piece from the garnished dish.

"Ummm.. Not bad. 6/10."

There was a glimpse of disappointment on our face.

"It's okay babies, I'm going to give both of you cooking lessons every weekend. Okay Mr.Bapat?? Off to Oxford after a couple of months, right???"

"Yehhh…….."

Time flew.. Aunty kept giving us cooking tips every weekend. Both of us were good cooks now. Thanks to the master chef Mrs. Bapat. For us cooking was just an excuse, the core reason was to spend time together. My cooking skills were now not only limited to making *upma* and noodles. But now *we* could also cook healthy home-made food which every Indian mom forcefully makes us eat.

CHAPTER FIFTEEN

Permanent Booking

5 months later

I had a stable routine in my Masters now. I was an intern in a research laboratory. Agastya and I regularly kept going on dates. And finally a time came when he proposed me. Right after the day his visa got approved. I had no idea about his plan to propose me. It was totally unexpected. The very next day his visa got approved, I got a text from Ags.

"Babe, wanna go on a date today? Discovered a new place in Bandra called Melaud"

"Too costly."

"Shut up, I'll pick you up by 7. Be ready"

"huh fine"

It was the first time we were going to a 5 star restaurant, probably because his visa got approved. I wonder what to wear. I had not even waxed my legs. But at last I wore a blue full sleeved one piece. Soft fabric with hugging curves, which turned out to make my butt look sexy. I felt the prettiest. I tied my hairs into a pony tail. To be honest that was not an appropriate outfit for dates. It felt more like a corporate meet up but if it makes me happy then it doesn't need to make sense to others.

Agastya was at the gate of my hostel already. Waitt why he's in a Honda City!! WOWW quite elegant.

"Madam, may I know who are you??"

"Excuse me?"

"Who's this? I'm waiting for my girlfriend. But seems like this princess deserves to travel in a grand pumpkin carriage the way Cinderella does. "

"Oh my god. Shut up Agastya. You scared me!"

"I really mean it. You look pretty like anything. This dress looks so pretty on you. Love your choices."

"Hmm... But look at yourself. You're no less than Prince Charming Henry. Let's rock it tonight!"

***

What is the first thing that comes to you mind when I say Mumbai?

Traffic... without any doubt.

The journey was more fun than the destination. Actually there's a small correction. I've started to realise that everything is fun when I'm with Agastya. I can even top a math exam if he's the teacher.

The journey was exclamatory. Everything is fun until it comes to our taste in music. Agastya is a bollywood fan whereas I am a Taylor's girl. But, I've learnt to vibe on bollywood music. As someone said 'Love is all about adjustment and sacrifice'.

I was not just in love with Agastya but also with his habits, behaviour, choices, and every single thing of his.

Finally we arrived at Agastya's suggested 5 star restaurant to spend money unnecessarily. As soon as we entered, I felt the presence of rich people. They were all dressed up like aristocrats. A guy in a black blazer walked toward us. It took me a moment to realize that he was the manager.

"Hey, we've reserved a table in the upper coach with the name Agastya Bapat"

"Yes sir, please come in.. follow that way" he said pointing towards the staircase."

After settling, I finally managed to speak in personal! "Agastya are you serious, you don't need to do all this.. It's way too expensive"

"I'm paying for it baby."

"So what!! Money is money. And what do you mean? I shouldn't be concerned about your money??"

"Aaru calm down.. It's a very big day for us. Tell me what would you like to have?"

I started analyzing the menu.. My eyes always fell on the right side of the column first.

"Don't look at the price baby" he said as if he caught me red handed.

"Fine!! Black bean cheese quesadillas, Mushroom risotto and a Blue ocean mojito"

Agastya placed our order and as soon as the food was brought to our table, he stood up from his chair and came towards me... He held my hand and asked "dance?"

And once again we danced; we danced exactly the way we did in my fresher's party eight years ago. But this time it was even more graceful. Our chemistry was even more organic now.

And there you go!! Finally the moment arrived, when he got onto his knees and said "Would you like to be concerned about my money for the rest of our lives?" That was a very abnormal thing to ask but I understood what he meant to say.

"Oh my god!! Are you kidding me! Shittt. Is this a dream? Pinch me!"

"Aaru..?"

"Oh yess wait.. Lemme digest first"

"I kick in sleep" I started the list of my habits, likes and dislikes. Wondering whether he would still stick to his decision.

"I can dodge" he replied

"I snore sometimes" I said

"I can listen to music." he replied

"I sleep till 12PM." I said

"I'll keep you awake all night" he replied

"I never finish my food." I said

"I love eating" he replied

"I don't like to exercise" I said

"Sex is a great exercise" he replied

"I hate walking" I said

"I would love to carry you" he replied

Everything was silent for a couple of seconds. People around us were so interested. I passed a huge signal of 'YES, MY DARLING BOY' to his eyes and they understood.

He stood up and offered a piece of key ring from his house keys to my ring finger.

"Are you serious???"

'Baby diamond ring was out of budget."

Both of us laughed diving into each other's eyes and we hugged.

Aristocrats around us stood up and started clapping and appreciating the young couple. It was no less than a bollywood film.

CHAPTER SIXTEEN

New Chapter

I couldn't believe that a time would come when we would be doing long distance. He was leaving for UK. Who said break-up hurts the most. Ever lived in a long distance relationship?

"Ahh, so you leaving me?"

"I have to. This is for us."

"I'll miss you."

"As if I won't. Darling, this has to be the time when you become your own best friend. The uncertainty is the weight we have to carry around. You want to be a Neuropsychologist; I want to be a Neurosurgeon. This is the time when we should realise that this is our life and we only have one chance to make it beautiful. Take out those fucking textbooks and study until the caffeine replaces the blood in your veins"

"I know right, but it's just that I've almost completed my masters now. And that's so depressing how we won't be able to see eachother in the upcoming years. I may sound selfish but...."

He interrupted and said "It's okay! I promise you to be all back soon. And I love you! That's all you wanted to hear. Am I right or Am I right?"

My face was partially covered with tears. I gave him a goofy look as soon as he leaned towards my face to kiss me. And that was the last time I saw him. I had no idea when we would see eachother again.

He bent down and took blessings of our parents as any Indian kid would do. It was the first time when my parents met Agastya after the official approval. HAHAHA.

Okay so he left. He boarded his flight and he took off. It was difficult but not impossible to not miss him.

Last year of my post graduation made my life hectic and I would like to be grateful for it.

There comes the final examination. I was a disturbed of course but Agastya was a person who has never affected my studies negatively.

***

1 year later

I was twenty four and in a one fine morning I received a mail.

"About what?"

About my placement in Harmony Hospital in Pune as a Jr. Neuropsychologist. I had applied for that job the previous week. The first person I informed this about was my parents. They were so happy! Then I called Agastya's parents that I'm soon shifting to Pune and finally texted Agastya.

"Hello Mr. Bapat! Received a mail this morning. I got a placement in Pune as a Junior Neuropsychologist. It's called the Harmony hospital."

"DAmM!! My girl capturing the world real quick!."

"hehehe. Tell me how's your college?"

"Quiet hectic. But somehow managing."

"Yeahh.."

Agastya and I were not in constant contact. But things never felt disconnected. They say Long distance doesn't work out but it does.
I guess. It did work out. It might give you sleepless nights and sleepy days if you're an over thinker.

Soon enough, I had to leave Varsha and my other Hostel mates. I shifted to Pune. New city, New personality, New beginnings, New everything. And suddenly I realised that dreams I was chasing started chasing me back.
Aarohi Mehta, You're finally a Neuropsychologist now!! That's the craziest thing which I wasn't able to consider a reality.

I was staying as a paid guest, after a week, I started going to my job. It was my first day. And as usual I did not know what to wear. I simply took out a pair of pants and a shirt to make a best try to look formal.

Remember the first day of your school, the day of your board examination, and the time you gave driving licence test. How was your feeling?
"Anxious?"
Exactly, that's what I felt.

I entered into the huge building and directly went to the reception. They sent me to Dr.Bose. A middle aged sweet confident lady. She had an amazing bright aura! Later, I got to know she was my boss.

After a warm discussion with her, I was permanently appointed and was paid more than what I expected!

So this is the life I dreamt for! THIS IS SO COOL!

I had got a common cabin and this was the only thing which didn't satisfy me. I wanted my own cabin. Like the seniors do. I had secretly declared a time period in which I wanted a grand promotion. 5 years!

"Are you sure?" I asked myself
"100%. By hook or crook" I replied.

CHAPTER SEVENTEEN

First Case

I start my first day at this prestigious hospital, eager to apply my knowledge and skills. My first patient Sarah, a 28 year old marketing executive, had been experiencing some memory lapses and confusion. She would forget conversations, misplace items, and struggle to recall familiar words. Her MRI and CT scans showed no sign of trauma and disease, leaving me to suspect a more complex cognitive case.

I sat in my office sipping morning coffee and reviewing the file of Sarah. As I dived deeper into Sarah's case, I uncovered a complex web of cognitive, emotional and psychological factors.

Sarah entered the office, I noticed her hesitated gait and furrowed brow. I begin her evaluation and administrated a series of tests to access Sarah's attention, memory, language, and problem solving skills. The results revealed a peculiar pattern of strengths and weaknesses. She excelled in creative tasks but struggled with logical reasoning. She was able to recall vivid details from childhood but forgot recent events.

I hypnotised that Sarah's brain was compensating for a hidden issue, possible related to her emotional past. I asked her about her personal life and she revealed a painful history of bullying and anxiety.

Over several sessions I helped her develop a personalized treatment plan, incorporating cognitive training, mindfulness techniques and emotional support. Sarah progress was remarkable; her memory loss improved and her confidence soared.

As I solved my first case, I realised that the human brain is dynamic, intricate puzzle. Every patient will present a unique challenge and every solution will require creativity, compassion and a deep understanding of the mind's complexities.

3 years later

I had been working for this hospital since three years now. I had established myself as a skilled clinician and researcher, earning the respect of my colleagues and the gratitude of my patients as well.

One day, my supervisor Dr.Bose, called me into her office:

"Aarohi, You've been doing outstanding work" she said. "I'm pleased to offer you a promotion to Senior Neuropsychologist.

I beamed with pride. The promotion meant more responsibilities, a higher salary, and a chance to lead my own research projects.

With my newfound financial stability, I began searching for my own apartment, I had been sharing a small condo with two roommates, but now I yearned for a place to call my own.

After weeks of browsing, I found a cosy 1bhk flat in a charming neighbourhood. I fell in love with the large windows, hardwood floor and the unique balcony overlooking a park.

As I signed the lease, I felt a sense of accomplishment over me. This apartment represented my independence, my hard work, and my commitment to my career.

The day I moved in, My parents gathered to celebrate. They talked and explored the new space, admiring my thoughtful decorations and the stunning view.

As I looked around at the people and the place I loved, I knew that this was just the beginning of my journey. I was eager to continue growing as a neuropsychologist, exploring the mysteries of the human brain, and creating a life filled with purpose and joy.

Agastya was nearly at the end of his post graduate studies. As he delved into his final research project, he couldn't help but feel proud of my accomplishments back home.

One evening, as we video-called, Agastya beamed with pride. "Aarohi,I heard about your promotion and a new apartment! You're crushing it, and I couldn't be more proud."

I blushed, feeling grateful for Agastya's unwavering support. "Thanks Ags. Your encouragement means everything to me. I can't wait for you to come back and celebrate with me in person"

Agastya's life in oxford was filled with intense study sessions, intricate lab work and stimulation discussions with colleagues. He spent his free time exploring the historic streets, punting along the River Cherwell, and trying local foods with his friends.

As he approached the end of his program, He felt a mix of emotions- excitement to reunite with our families and me, but also a tinge of sadness to leave behind the incredible experience and friendships he'd made in Oxford.

Our regular video calls kept us close, sharing stories of our days and supporting each other's passions. Agastya would often share his experience in the lab, and I would discuss my latest research project.

With his return imminent, Agastya began making plans for our future together. He couldn't wait to reunite and build a future filled with love, laughter and a shared passion for neuroscience.

As Agastya packed his bags, he smiled knowing that he was coming home to a strong, accomplished woman who inspired him every day. I too, felt my heart filled with joy. Eagerly awaiting Agastya's return and the chapter we would began together.

CHAPTER EIGHTEEN

India!

Agastya stepped off the plane in Mumbai, My heart was filled with excitement. I had missed him terribly, and the thought of reuniting made every moment of our long journey worthwhile.

As he made his way through customs, my phone buzzed with a text from Agastya "just landed. Can't wait to see you!"

I smiled, my eyes scanning the crowded airport for a glimpse of Agastya's bright smile. And then I saw him. I waved enthusiastically.

We embraced tightly, the world around us melting away. I breathed in the familiar scent of Agastya's perfume, feeling like he was finally home.

After meeting his parents, the next day I took him to Pune!
The drive to my apartment was a blur of laughter and catching up. Agastya marvelled at the new decorations and the cosy atmosphere I had created.

Over a romantic dinner we talked about everything and nothing- our dreams, aspirations and plans for the future together. Agastya shared stories from Oxford and I filled him in my office gossips.

As the night drew to close, he took my hand, his eyes locked on mine. "I've missed you so much" he whispered. "I promise to never be away from you for so long again."

My heart skipped a beat "I've missed you too." I replied. My voice was barely above a whisper. "I love you Agastya"

"I love you too Aarohi" Agastya said, his lips brushing against mine in a tender kiss.

As we sat together on the couch, watching the stars twinkle over Pune, we both knew that this was just the beginning of our new chapter together.

Agastya started applying for jobs in Pune, where I was working. We wanted to be close to eachother and build life together.

Meanwhile, I was excelling in my career, working as a psychologist. I was happy to have Agastya in the same city, and we could finally spend quality time with eachother.

Agastya landed a job in a reputed hospital in Pune, and we both breathed a sigh of relief. We could now finally balance our professional and personal life.

But, ever heard Indian relatives minding their own business?

Agastya's relative aunt Rukmani called him with disapproval. "Agastya, what's wrong with you? You're staying at you girlfriend's apartment, shamelessly living together without marriage. What will people think?

Agastya sighed, used to his aunt's taunts "Aunty we're adults, and we can make our own decisions.

But she wouldn't stop. "And what about the chance in England and earning in dollars? You were selected for a prestigious fellowship, and you gave it up for.......this?" She gestured to my apartment. "You are sacrificing your future for nothing."

Agastya took a deep breath. "Aunty, I want to serve for my own country, not work for someone else's. I prefer to stay connected to my roots and make a difference here."

Aunty Rukmani scoffed "Roots? You're being foolishly sentimental. England offered you a chance at a world class career, amd you threw it away.

Agastya's voice became firm "Aunty I'd rather make a difference in India, where I'm needed. I won't abandon my country for personal gain.

I, who was quietly listening, spoke up "Agastya's decision shows his commitment to his values and his country. We're proud to be together and build a life here."

Aunt *Rukmani* huffed, but we remained firm, knowing that our love and choices were stronger than any criticism.

***

Our days were filled with work, but we made sure to spend evenings together. We would have dinner together, go for walks or watch movies. On weekends, we would explore Pune together, visiting new places and trying out new foods. We were each other's rock, supporting and motivating eachother to reach new heights.

I would often attend Agastya's hospital events and he would accompany me with my research files. We were proud of each other's accomplishments and celebrated every success.

As our relationship grew stronger, we started making long term plans. We started about getting married, buying a bigger home, and travelling somewhere together.

CHAPTER NINETEEN

Planning

Agastya and I sat together, holding hands, and discussed our future. "We're not getting younger, and we've achieved stability in our careers" Agastya said "I think it's time we get married"

I nodded in agreement "I'm ready too, let's talk to our parent and start the planning"

We decided to meet both the parents together, to share the news. At my place, in Gandhinagar, We sat our parents and began the conversation.

"Mom, Dad, we wanted to talk to you about our future" I started

"Aarohi and I have decided to get married." Agastya added

Our parents exchanged a knowing glance, smiling. "We're thrilled beta! We were waiting for this day."

The four parents, Agastya and me sat together and started discussing the dates, venue and guest lists. We decided a beautiful winter wedding in Goa. With mixed of both the traditional elements.

Our marriage planning was a dream come true. I had always wanted a beach wedding, and Goa's stunning coastline offered a perfect setting.

We decided on a beautiful sea facing resort with crystal-clear water and powdery white sand. The resort's wedding planner Maria helped us coordinate every detail.

First, we finalised the guest lists, keeping it intimate with close family and friend. Agastya's parents were thrilled to invite their Maharastrian community; my parents welcomed our Gujarati community.

Next, they chose a stunning beachside mandap for the ceremony, adorned with seashells, flowers, and greenery. I selected a gorgeous bridal outfit while Agastya opted for a light, airy kurta and dhoti.

To be honest, the first challenge arose when deciding the destination. My family wanted a beach wedding in Goa, while Agastya's family insisted on a traditional temple wedding in Pune. After a playful blunter they finally compromised and decided Goa as the final option.

Next, they tackled the menu. My mother wanted to serve traditional Gujarati dishes like *undhiyu and puri* whereas Agastya's mother insisted her favourites like *Misal pav* and *puran poli.*
We decided to have a fusion of both the cuisines.

As the weeding approached, the families got into more playful squabbles. My family teased Agastya for his *Garba* moves, while Agastya's family joked about my cooking skills.

***

As the countdown begins. I was getting married in less than ten days!! We had arrived in Goa. Excited for the celebrations. The *sangeet* night was a highlight, with both families dancing and singing together under the stars.

I couldn't take it anymore, the endless rituals, the constant scrutiny, the fake smile. I needed a break and I needed Agastya. I texted him to meet me on the beach at 5AM, before the chaos began again.

Agastya sensing my distress arrived early, carrying a thermos of hot coffee and a blanket. He found me sitting on the bench, watching the waves.

"Hey what's wrong?" he asked sitting by my side

I sighed, "I just can't take it Agastya. The rituals, the expectations... I feel like I'm losing myself in all this"

Agastya put his arm around me, pulling me close. "We'll get through this together, Aaru. We'll make our own way, own rules. We don't have to conform to the society's expectations."

I smiled feeling a weight lift off my shoulders. "I love you Ags"

"I love you too Aarohi. More than anything" As the sun rises over the ocean, we sat together in comfortable silence, watching the waves roll in. For a moment everything else faded away, and all that mattered was our love for eachother.

We decided to walk along the beach. We strolled hand in hand, feeling the soft sand between the toes and gentle oceanic breeze in the hair.

As we walked, we talked about dreams and aspirations. We talked about our work life and shared each other's family gossips.

Agastya stopped and turned towards me. He took my face in his hands, his eyes locking into mine.

"I'm so proud of the person you are, Aaru!" he said. His voice filled with emotions "You light up my world in ways I never thought possible"

My heart skipped a beat. I felt the same about Agastya-his kindness, his intelligence; his compassion inspired me every day.

As we stood there, the waves crashing against the shore. Agastya leaned in and kissed me softly. The world around us melted away leaving only two of us, lost in magic of our love. We stood there for a moment, wrapped in each other's arms, feeling the love and connection that only we shared.

CHAPTER TWENTY

Finally!

The sun rose over the Goan horizon, casting a warm glow over the beachside resort where we our wedding preparation was in full swing. The air was alive with the sweet scent of frangipani and the sound of gentle waves crashing the shore.

I woke up early, feeling like a princess. My mother and the bridesmaids helped me get ready, their hands trembling with excitement as they adored me with delicate jewellery and a garland of fresh flowers.

Meanwhile, Agastya stood calmly in front of the mirror, his eyes stunning with happiness as he adjusted his kurta and dhoti. His father and groomsmen surrounded him, their faces beaming with pride.

As the guests begin to arrive, the atmosphere became electric. The sound of the *shehnai* filled the air, and the aroma of delicious food wafted from the catering department.

The ceremony began with Agastya's procession, accompanied by his friends and family, dancing and singing to the beats of *dhol!* I watched them from the balcony upstairs. My heart was overflowing with love and joy.

As Agastya reached the *mandap,* I gave my grand entry along with the bridesmaid. Our eyes met and time stood still. The priest began the rituals, and we finally exchanged the vows and sealed our love with a kiss. We shared a gaze that spoke volumes. It was a look of triumph, of joy, and of disbelief. We both thought to ourselves, "We did it! We're finally getting married!"

As we gazed into each other's eyes, they couldn't help but reminisce about the first time we met. In the fresher's party, where we danced together on *Janam Janam*. Who would have thought that carefree night would lead to a lifetime of love and happiness?

My mind wandered back to the day, remembering hoe Agastya had spun me around a twirled me to the music. I had felt a spark of connection, but never thought it would blossom into something more.

As we stood there, holding hands and looking into each other's eyes, we both knew that our love was meant to be. We had come a long way since that fresher's party and we were excited to see what the future held for us.

The moment of truth arrived as Agastya applied *sindoor* to my forehead, sealing our union forever. The guests erupted in cheers and applause as they embraced, *now husband and wife!*

The reception, that followed was a vibrant celebration of our love, with food, drink and music flowing freely..

As the night wore on, we were surrounded with our loved ones, basking in the happiness and blessing the filled air. Our wedding day was a dream comes true.

Our first dance as husband and wife was a romantic sway to classic bollywood ballad. We moved in perfect harmony, our eyes locked on eachother, as if nothing else existed. As we danced, the lights around us twinkled like stars, casting a magical glow over the entire scene. It was as if the universe itself was blessing the family's union.

After the dance, Agastya and I made our way to buffet, where we were greeted with a sumptuous spread of Gujarati and Maharastrian cuisine. We savoured each bite, enjoying the textures of the dishes, and the company of eachother.

The best part comes when the clock struck the midnight. We were told to visit the beach where a surprise party was awaited for us by our college friends. They had made a set up of a beautiful firework display, which lit up the night sky with vibrant colours and patterns.

CHAPTER TWENTY-ONE

Vacation

After the wedding, Agastya and I chose the picturesque hill station of Shimla as our honeymoon destination. We wanted a romantic gateway amidst nature's beauty, and Shimla offered the perfect blend of serenity, adventure and romance.

Our journey began with a scenic train ride from Mumbai to Shimla, where we enjoyed the breathtaking views of Himalayas. Upon arrival, we checked into a cosy little cottage with a stunning view of the valley

Days were spent exploring Shimla's charm hand-in-hand. We strolled through the Mall road, visiting quaint shops and cafes, and marvelling at the colonial architecture. We took a romantic walk to the nearby *Jakhu temple*, watching the sunset behind the Himalayas.

One day, we embarked on thrilling trek to the Chadwick falls, surrounded by lush green forests and chirping birds. We picnicked by the waterfall, sharing stories and laughter.

In the evening, we cuddled up by the fireplace, sipping hot chocolate/. We enjoyed the candlelit dinners at local restaurants, savouring *Himachali* cuisine and wine.

As the honeymoon drew to close- I planned a surprise for Agastya-a hot air balloon ride over Shimla hills, where we galloped like royalty, taking in the majestic views. We even visited the famous Kufri fun world, where we laughed and played like kids enjoying the thrill rides and games.

Shimla was a perfect blend of adventure, romance, and relaxation. As we returned home, we knew that our love had grown stronger and our marriage was off to a beautiful start.

Now, it was a time to reconnect back to the reality check in Pune where our duties were waiting for us.

CHAPTER TWENTY-TWO

Life

After returning from our dreaming honeymoon, we settled into a comfortable routine in Pune. Our days began with gentle morning ritual where we would wake up together, enjoy a warm cup of tea and get ready for work. We would then head to the hospital for our shift.

In the evening we would cook dinner together, experimenting new recipes and flavours. We would spend quality time simply by watching movies, playing cards or simply cuddling on the couch.

On weekends we would clean the house and explore the countryside of Pune. We would often take eachother on surprise outings, like a sudden trip to nearby hill or an office party. I would always surprise him with a weekend trip to Mumbai to meet *Aai-Baba*.

Our routine was a perfect balance of work, play and love. We prioritised our relationship, making time for eachother amidst their busy schedules. As we settled into the married life.

1 year later

Our first fight was after a year. It was quit matured and nuanced one. We had grown up together, learned each other's quirks, and developed a deeper understanding of our relation.

It started with a discussion about his future plan. Agastya wanted to build up his own hospital in Mumbai, while I hesitated to leave Pune. We had different opinions and our conversation became a debate.

He felt that I was being too attached to my job and wasn't considering his goals. I felt that he was being too focused in his career and not focusing my needs. Our discussion turned into a heated, with both of us raising voices.

"I feel like you're holding me back. I need to get this opportunity" He said

"I feel like you're abandoning me Agastya. I need you here, with me"

We realised that this fight wasn't about building his own hospital. It was about our insecurities. We took a break, cooled down, and had a calmer conversation.

At the end I was the one who compromised, we decided that we would shift back to Mumbai, and Agastya would build his own hospital.

After settling into our new life in Mumbai, Agastya's career as a neurosurgeon flourished. He began for his exceptional skills and innovative approaches to complex neurological cases. Encouraged by his success, he decided to finally start building a state-of-the-art neuroscience hospital.

With the help of the investors and his own savings, Agastya founded "NeuroSphere"- a cutting edge hospital dedicated to advanced neurological care and research. He poured his heart and soul into this project, ensuring that every aspect of the hospital reflected his vision of compassionate and excellence-driven care.

As NeuroSphere began to take shape, Agastya knew he needed talent team to bring his vision to life. He turned to me giving me an offer to lead the neuropsychology department and research lab. With my expertise in cognitive psychology and research experience, I agreed this proposal. Because why not?

Under my supervision, the neuropsychology department and the research lab became a hub of the groundbreaking research and excellent patient care. Our partnership flourished, both personally and professionally as we worked together to make NeuroSphere a beacon of hope for those affected by neurological disorders.

Our collaboration sparked new ideas and approaches, combining Agastya's surgical expertise and my knowledge of cognitive psychology. We began to develop novel treatments and therapies, pushing the boundaries of neuroscience and improving lives.

As NeuroSphere grew, so did our reputation as a powerhouse couple in the field of neuroscience. We became sought- after speakers, researchers, and clinicians, known for innovative approaches and dedication to excellence.

At last. , Sacrificing Pune was a good decision.

CHAPTER TWENTY-THREE

Big newzz

After achieving immense success with NeuroSphere, we decided to expand impact beyond the hospital walls. We established "NeuroSphere Foundation" a non-profit organization dedicated to promoting neuroscience education, research and community outreach.

We had launched initiatives such as *Mind Matters, Neuro Genius and Brain wave.*

Our foundation also partnered with colleges to develop curriculum focused neuroscience program, inspiring the next generation for this field. Our success with NeuroSphere and foundation caught the attention of global leaders in healthcare and education. We were also invited to speak in national conferences, sharing our vision and expertise with broader audience.

Later on, we collaborated in a project called "NeuroSpark" which focused on developing diagnosed tools, personalised therapies, and neurostimulation devices.

Throughout the journey, we remained committed to our core values: COMPASSION, EXCELLENCE, and INNOVATION.
We continued to inspire and empower eachother.

***

My heart trembled as I held the pregnancy test, my heart racing with excitement and nervousness. I suspected it for weeks, but now it was official. I was going to be a mother!!!!

I couldn't wait to share the news with Agastya, but I wanted to make it special. I planned a special dinner at home cooking his favourite dishes and setting up a romantic atmosphere.

As he walked in, exhausted from a long day at NeuroSphere, I greeted him with a warm smile "Hey love! I've a surprise for you"

His eyes lit up, and he followed me to the dining area. The candles, flowers and aroma of his favourite food caught him off guard "Aaru what is all this?"

I took his hand trembling. "Ags, I have something to tell you. Something amazing"

He locked his eyes into mine, sensing the excitement "What is it?"

I took a deep breath. "We're pregnant, Mr.Agastya Bapat we're having a baby!"

His face froze, and then erupted into a wide smile. He swept me into his arms, twirling me around the room. "Oh my god, this is incredible"

The joyful screams and laughter filled the room as we hugged, tears of happiness streaming down our faces.

The next day, we shared the news with our parents, who were overjoyed. *Aai* couldn't stop crying into happy tears. "My grandchild is coming!! I'm going to be a grandma!!"

Ma beamed in pride, "My baby is having a baby! I'm going to be a *Nani!!*"

Our fathers, both strong and supportive men, exchanged warm smiles. "Our families are growing. We couldn't be happier for both of you"

The grandparents to be showered us with blessings, love, and advice, eagerly awaiting the arrival of the new family member.

As we celebrated, Agastya whispered into my ears. "Our love is growing and our family is expanding. I couldn't ask for more"

I smiled, my hear full. "Me neither, my love, me neither".

CHAPTER TWENTY-FOUR

Journey

My pregnancy journey was a whirlwind of emotions, challenges and joy. As a partner of NeuroSpark and NeuroSphere, I was determined to manage our company while ensuring my health and well-being. Agastya and our families were my rock, providing unwavering support and care.

Initially, I continued to work tirelessly, hiding my morning sickness and fatigue. However, as my pregnancy progressed, I realised the importance of self care. I delegated tasks, prioritized my health, and took regular breaks.

Agastya became my personal assistant, chef and massage therapist, ensuring I ate nutritious food, exercised gently and rested adequately.

Both families were overjoyed and supportive, offering help in every possible way. Ma moved in to help me with household chores, while *Aai* cooked nutritious meals and both of them shared wisdom on motherhood together. Both the fathers provided emotional support, offering words of encouragement and reassurance.

As my belly grew, my team rallied around me, taking on additional responsibilities and ensuring a seamless transition. Agastya, being the lovely husband, was always available to lend a helping hand.

Together, we navigated the ups and downs of pregnancy, embracing each milestone with joy and gratitude. My health and well-being became the top priority and flourished under the love and care of my support system.

As we all awaited the arrival of the little one, we felt grateful for our journey, knowing that our love, family and support would guide us through the adventures of parenthood.

Few moths later

My labour pain started on a sunny Saturday morning. Agastya, who had been preparing for this moment suddenly, overcame with anxiety. He paced back and forth in the hospital room, coaching me through breathing exercises while trying to stay calm his own nerves.

As the contractions intensified, my focus turned inward, and I began to push. Agastya was now pale and sweaty; he held my hands whispering the words of encouragement.

Finally, after what seemed like an eternity, out **daughter** was born. The doctor held up the tiny, squirming bundle, and Agastya's eyes winded in awe.

"It's a girl!!" The doctor announced.

Agastya's face contorted in a mix of emotions- shock, joy, and fear. He stumbled backward, collapsing onto the couch, and buried his face in his hands.

I was exhausted but radiant, smiled weakly at my husband. "Agastya, meet our daughter"

As the nurse placed the baby in my arms, Agastya slowly rose, his eyes fixed on the tiny creature. Tears streamed down his face as he gazed at his daughter for the first time.

Both the families buzzed into the room, eager to meet the new addition. Aai kissed the baby's forehead while Ma whispered blessings into her ear.

As we gazed at the baby girl, we knew we had found the perfect name- **Yashna.**

"That's me!! That's me!!!!"

"Yes Yashna!! That's you. My baby girl. That was the day best day of my life, when God placed you in my arms"

"I love you Ma, tell me what happened next."

We chose this name, because your arrival marked the triumph of our love, success of our journey together and beginning of a new chapter in our lives.

As we gazed at you, we knew that our lives would never be the same, and we couldn't wait to watch you grow and flourish.

Yashna's eyes sparkles as Aarohi finished telling the story of her parent's journey, from their chance encounter to the birth of their beautiful daughter- Yashna!

She smiled, feeling grateful for the love and support that has always surrounded her.

"And that's how my parents met eachother, and fell in love" she concluded.

The story is a reminder that true love can conquer all and that family is not just about blood ties, but also the bond we create with eachother. .

"So that's how you met my father," Yashna Bapat said with a grin, *"the man who would become the rock of our family and the love of my mother's life."*

Yashna's Note

Dear Readers,

I hope you enjoyed my parent's love story. How they met and fell in love. It's a testament to the power of true love and determination.

My mother, Aarohi Mehta, had her first crush in school, but life had other plans. And they turned out to be the best ones. She went on to build a successful career, and that's where she found her prince charming. Agastya Bapat- My dad. Their story taught me valuable lessons:

1. **Dedication towards career:** My mother's focus on her love didn't distract her from career; instead it led her to the right person. Why? Because she had fixed her priorities.

1. **Success:** Their individual success made their relationship stronger. They balanced each other's strengths and weaknesses, proving that, together we can achieve more.

3. **Overcoming obstacles**: Life threw challenges their way, but they found each other, showing me that with perseverance, we can overcome anything.

4. **Embracing uncertainty:** My mother's journey showed me that life is unpredictable, but with an open heart and mind, we can find our ways.

Their story inspires me to work hard, believe in love, and stay true to myself. I learned that with determination and resilience, I can overcome obstacles and find my own prince charming.

Thank you Mom, Dad, for being my role models and showing me the true meaning of love and success.

With love and appreciation,

Yashna Bapat. <3

Author's Note

Dear Readers,

As I wrote the love story of Aarohi and Agastya, I sought to convey a deeper message beyond the confines of romance. Their journey is a testament to the transformative power of humanism, where both individuals embrace each other's strengths and weaknesses without the shackles of ego or social expectations.

Their relationship is a beautiful dance of mutual respect, trust and partnership. They effortlessly balance their professional pursuits with domestic responsibilities, never once compromising on their individuality or love for eachother.

Through this story, I aimed to highlight the importance of equality in relationships, not in the sense of seeking equal rights, but in the sense of embracing equal responsibilities.

Aarohi and Agastya's bond is built on the foundation of mutual support, where both of them work hand in hand sharing the burdens and joys of life together.

This is not a tale of feminism, but of humanism- celebration of the human sprit's capability for love, empathy and understanding. It is a reminder that relationships thrive when we shed our ego, embrace our vulnerabilities, and work together as equal.

I always believe that stories play a huge influence on people. And therefore, my story is a powerful reminder that a perfect society is possible when we prioritize humanism, empathy, and understanding.

May the journey of Aarohi and Agastya inspire the readers to cultivate meaningful connections, built on the principals of mutual respect, trust and equal partnership.

Note: This story is a complete work of imagination and fiction. Any resemblance to actual events, individuals or organisations is purely coincidental and unintentional. The characters, plot, and settings are entirely fictional and not meant to represent or reference any real person, place or incident

Love,
Tulsi Davey